**Penguin Books**

# Bewitched

Isla Fisher was born in 1976, in the old walled city of Muscat in the Sultanate of Oman. She was the last non-Arab to be born there. She travelled for some years in Asia before settling with her Scottish family in Western Australia. She was educated at Methodist Ladies College in Perth and spent many of her schooldays, from thirteen years upwards, on various film sets. She left home halfway through year twelve to take up a part in 'Paradise Beach', filmed on the Gold Coast of Queensland. Six months later she joined the cast of 'Home and Away', where she is still a regular.

Isla lives in Sydney and frequently returns to Perth to visit her parents and four brothers. Her hobbies are horse riding, writing and reading.

Also by Isla Fisher:

*Seduced by Fame*

# BEWITCHED

## isla fisher
### with Elspeth Reid

**Penguin Books**

Puffin Books
Penguin Books Australia Ltd
487 Maroondah Highway, PO Box 257
Ringwood, Victoria 3134, Australia
Penguin Books Ltd
Harmondsworth, Middlesex, England
Viking Penguin, A Division of Penguin Books USA Inc.
375 Hudson Street, New York, New York 10014, USA
Penguin Books Canada Limited
10 Alcorn Avenue, Toronto, Ontario, Canada M4V 3B2
Penguin Books (N.Z.) Ltd
182–190 Wairau Road, Auckland 10, New Zealand

First published by Penguin Books Australia, 1995
1 3 5 7 9 10 8 6 4 2
Copyright © Isla Fisher and Elspeth Reid, 1995

Typeset in 11.5/14pt Times Roman by Midland Typesetters
Printed in England by Clays Ltd, St Ives plc

National Library of Australia
Cataloguing-in-Publication data:

Fisher, Isla, 1976– .
Bewitched
ISBN 0 14 025575 3.
I. Title. (Series: Live the fantasy).

A823.3

*To my father and stepfather.*
*Fortunately I have never had to search for either*
*They are always there for me.*

# A note about Russian names

Every Russian has three names: a first name, a patronymic and a surname. The patronymic is the father's first name with a suffix added - 'ovich' meaning 'son of', or 'ovna' meaning 'daughter of'.

For example, a man whose first name is 'Alexander', names his son 'Stefan Alexandrovich' ('Stefan, son of Alexander') plus, of course, the surname.

In turn, Stefan Alexandrovich names his son 'Nikolai Stefanovich' ('Nikolai, son of Stefan'), and his daughter 'Anna Stefanovna' ('Anna, daughter of Stefan').

Russians usually call each other by both first name and patronymic. For example, a teacher in a Russian classroom would never say just 'Anna' when speaking to a student - she would always call her 'Anna Stefanovna'. Likewise at work, workmates would not just say 'Nikolai' - they would call him 'Nikolai Stefanovich'. Only within the family would people use just the first name. Surnames are rarely used as a form of address.

**1**

Valentina chewed her lip anxiously. Somewhere, down there, her mother was watching – sitting upright, pen poised, ready to note every false step.

A familiar bar of music drew her back to the stage where Romeo stood in the spotlight, motionless as a Greek statue, his muscular body proud against the moonlit backdrop. Prokofiev's violin sobbed and soared from the velvet-black auditorium. Taking a deep breath, she lifted up on to *pointe* and floated out on the stage. Romeo waited, arms outstretched, his strong thighs braced to catch her as she flew into his arms.

The music swelled as they moved through the first *adagio* of the *pas-de-deux*. She became Juliet, turning in the circle his hands made around her waist, then falling back so low her head brushed the stage, one leg extended gracefully. Now she was upright, facing him. Then a long intense

*1*

moment, eyes locked, the lightest of kisses, before he swept her up into the air like a chiffon doll, spiralling, twisting, free-falling back into his arms.

On the other side of the stage, a shadow fell. Distracted, she narrowed her eyes, making out the silhouette of a man. She'd seen him in the wings before.

What did he want?

'Hold it, mate.' A man's voice rang out from the technicians' gallery. 'Got a problem with the central spots. Can you take a break for five minutes?'

'Sure.' Romeo became Ben in an instant. 'I need to cool down. Coming for some water, Val?'

'No, I'll just stay here and work on my extensions. You go.'

Ben ran a hand through his damp blond hair and shrugged. 'Robo-dancer! Do you ever let up?'

High heels approached, tapping a warning on the empty stage. Valentina straightened, tense and expectant.

'My dears!' Madame Galliano appeared in the spotlight, dressed entirely in purple, stretching out her jewelled hands. 'That was wonderful!' The anxious line on Valentina's forehead relaxed.

'But Ben, you must handle her more gently. She is a precious object, a virgin, the light of your life. Not a surfboard to fling over your shoulder!' 'Like this,' she added, as she held an imaginary lover in her arms. Valentina thought she saw a flicker of something like pain in her eyes.

'Now, my little Tina.' She turned to Valentina, her voice hardening. 'You must hold the arabesque longer, child. You must stay on *pointe*!'

'But Mama, my right toe is swollen. If I hold it more than thirty seconds, it'll collapse. The whole trip could be cancelled.'

Madame patted her cheek. 'Never! You will go, and you will feel no pain, at least not on stage. And you will hold your arabesques at least forty-five seconds. I say so. Now, I go. I see you both in the Green Room for notes at the end of Act Two.' She strode back to her seat in the front stalls.

Ben reached for a towel and rubbed his chest vigorously. 'The original dragon woman! If she wasn't your mother – and the best ballet teacher in Sydney – I'd ...'

'Well, she is, and without her where would either of us be?'

'Married,' Ben laughed, 'living in my caravan, and I'd be surfing the competitions to support you.'

'Ridiculous! I'd never marry a surfie, and in any case I've got my career.' She looked up sternly before slipping off her shoe and adjusting the padding around her toe. 'And she's right about the arabesques!' A tiny drop of blood spotted the cotton padding. She winced and replaced her shoe.

Ben peered into the dark auditorium. 'There she is, lurking in the dark, notebook in hand, taking down every minute detail in that spidery writing of hers. Are you sure she didn't spy for the KGB in Russia?'

'Only when they didn't hold their arabesques. Come on, Ben, we should be working.' She turned wearily towards the balcony. Obedience and Discipline. The words were engraved on her heart – habits she no longer questioned. Her feet might ache from endless rehearsals and classes, but her resolution never wavered.

'One minute more,' came the call from lighting.

Ben picked up the rubber sword from the fight scene with Tybalt. He slashed it several times in the air, arm held high like a French courtier. Then, suddenly leaping forward, he plunged it under her arm, in the classic stage *coup-de-grâce*. Valentina stifled a giggle, moaned dramatically and crumpled delicately onto the stage.

'That's enough nonsense!' Madame's voice spliced the air. 'Discipline and Obedience,' she rapped. Then the music rose, recalling the balcony scene. Romeo and Juliet took their places and fell in love for the fifteenth time that day.

It was almost six o'clock when her mother finally let them escape to shower. Valentina stripped off gratefully, enjoying the stinging heat easing the pain in her limbs. As the water cascaded over her back, she unpicked the plaits she had knotted into a bun with elastic bands. She envied the other dancers their fine silky hair. Her heavy mane of springing ebony curls was impossible to control without severe plaiting and thousands of hair grips. Free at last, she massaged her throbbing scalp and poured on dollops of banana conditioner to smooth out the tangles.

The changing room was damp with tropical-scented steam by the time she towelled off and pulled on her old tracksuit and sneakers. A final rub sent her hair into wild curls around her face. Unhappy with the effect, she pulled it tidily back into a scrunchy before meticulously replacing everything in her locker. Her 'Juliet' costume, a wisp of filmy chiffon scattered with white rosebuds, had to be returned to the wardrobe mistress. She switched off the lights in the changing rooms and set off down the dimly-lit corridor to Wardrobe.

'Valentina?'

Startled, she flattened against the wall, blinking to adjust her eyes. The light was faint, but she could make out the man she'd seen earlier. The watcher. How on earth did he know her name?

'Excuse me. I saw you dance just now. Are you from the Academy?' His deep voice echoed in the darkness like an underwater bell. And there was an accent; was it an English accent?

'No – I – what do you want?' Valentina was surprised to hear the tremor in her voice.

'You look like a Russian gipsy.'

'What are you talking about? I'm Australian.' Her voice was a scared whisper.

'No,' he said. 'Your eyes, and your mouth . . . like a Byzantine Madonna. Who are your parents?'

'Madame Galliano. She runs the Academy. We're rehearsing here ... please, leave me alone.' She twisted her head sideways.

'I won't harm you. I only want to talk to you.' His dark, hooded eyes burnt into her own.

'Please,' she whispered, 'let me go.'

But he made no move to go. He spoke her name slowly, rolling the syllables like music, 'Va-len-tin-a.'

'Back off, mate.' Ben materialised out of the shadows, slipping his body between them. 'In this country the lady has to give permission.'

The man stared at Valentina. 'I don't need permission to talk. I only ask a few questions.'

'Bullshit.' Ben leaned back against the wall, arms folded. 'Now apologise for upsetting her.' His voice was low, but there was steel in his manner.

'Apologise?' The man glared at Ben. 'As a student from the Academy, you should be careful how you address me! Do you know who I am?' He curled his lip in disdain.

Ben straightened, his full shoulders inches higher. 'I don't give a stuff who you are ...'

'It's all right, Ben.' She grabbed his hand and ducked sideways, pulling him after her. 'Leave it.' Ben followed her out into the corridor.

They ran into the wardrobe mistress carrying armloads of costumes. 'Have you seen Sasha? Dark guy, wild hair.'

Ben nodded. 'I almost thumped him. The dickhead put the hard word on Vally.'

Her eyes popped. 'Are you sure? That doesn't sound like him. Well, I hope you're not looking for a job next year with this company, then. He's Sasha Speransky – the new choreographer!'

'What!' Valentina stopped dead in her tracks. 'Oh, Ben – and you nearly decked him!'

'Too right. Teach him to bail you up in a dark corner.'

Valentina frowned. 'Oh, God! It's a good job we're leaving next week. They're probably sick of us using their stage to rehearse; we don't want any complaints. Promise you won't tell Mama about this. She'll burst a blood vessel. She's strung so tightly at the moment she could snap.'

'It's your business.' He held open the foyer door. 'Ah, Madame, here we both are.' He switched on a welcoming grin, bowing slightly and ignoring the kick Valentina aimed at his ankle.

Madame was standing in the red-carpeted entrance of Her Majesty's Theatre, rapping out instructions to the stage manager. She turned querulously at their arrival, her mouth a purple slit.

'Why so late?'

'I had a spot of bother; Val rescued me,' said Ben. Then he held open the door.

Madame led them out into a warm, humid evening. Queen palms thrashed against the street lights, throwing strange shadows on the pavement. 'The storm is coming. You want a lift, Ben?'

'Got the ute, thanks. I'm going straight down to Bronte – there'll be three-metre swells tonight.'

Madame muttered in Russian, then said to him, 'Break one bone, any bone, and I'll personally break the rest. Understood? We have no under-studies, and I've given my blood for this trip. Nothing will stop it.' But she smiled fondly after him all the same.

Valentina watched him disappear. If only her mother would accept her the way she accepted Ben, respecting him, letting him go his own way. As long as he worked well on stage, she forgave him everything else. With her it was different.

On the drive home she listened in silence to a stream of advice. 'On the fourth bar of the second movement,' said Madame, tapping out the rhythm with her purple nails on the steering wheel, 'move out on your right foot. La-la-la-la . . . ' She sang out the melody, interrupting herself as she thought of more instructions.

Valentina closed her eyes in the darkness, pic-turing Ben alone in the crashing waves. She sent out a silent prayer he wouldn't get hurt. That man must have rattled her more than she realised. Why was she worrying about Ben now, after all these years? He'd been born a kamikaze and he'd never had an accident yet.

The wind was howling like a grey wolf by the time they reached home, a small brick house in a cul-de-sac of small brick houses. Valentina hated the claustrophobic streets, the bay windows with net curtains staring relentlessly at each other, and the identical gardens, like open prisons for plants.

Babushka, her grandmother, was stirring soup in the kitchen when they arrived home. Firelight danced on the antique porcelain arranged on an old oak dresser. Black and white photographs of her mother dancing hung on every wall; *Swan Lake*, *Les Sylphides*, *La Dame aux Camélias*. Choral music from Chesnokov filled the room.

'Must we listen to this funeral dirge?' Madame snapped off the stereo and flicked the TV remote. An over-excited games show host was yelling as a wall-mounted casino wheel slowed to a halt. 'Tina-lina, my vodka, please!'

Sighing, Valentina kissed her grandmother's cheek and reached for the exquisite Bohemian crystal her mother used for her evening drink. It was as much a part of her as the heavy gold charm bracelets and ruby rings. She thought of the man in the theatre. Shivering, she twisted the cap off the vodka bottle.

'*Vanuchka*, are you okay? The toe, she okay?' Her grandmother peered at her anxiously. Anxiety was a drug to Babushka; she'd taken it all her life and was completely addicted.

'I'm fine. Mama wants me to hold on *pointe*, but I'll be fine.'

An imperious voice rang out. 'My vodka!'

Valentina carried over the tall amethyst glass.

'My tiny Tina,' she said, casting sorrowful eyes towards her daughter, 'Where are my vinegar 'n ketchup chips? You know I love to nibble them with my vodka.' But she accepted the drink graciously, slipped off her black stilettos and tucked her silky legs under the wide purple skirt.

'I haven't had time to pick up the shopping,' Valentina muttered. 'Maybe tomorrow . . .'

Babushka handed Valentina a yoghurt and pointed to the pot of bubbling beetroot soup. Outside the wind whipped and rattled the window panes. Valentina stirred the creamy yoghurt into the soup, watching the swirls grow pink.

'Babushka, are there a lot of gipsies in Russia?'

Her grandmother was frying chicken, slitting her eyes against the hissing fat. 'Too many.'

'What do they look like?'

'Why you ask a question like that?' She looked sharply sideways at Valentina, her mouth tightening into a nervous purse.

A burst of cheering thundered from the TV. Valentina whispered into Babushka's ear. 'Today, a man stopped me at the theatre. He said I looked like a Russian gipsy. Like a Byzantine Madonna. What did he mean?'

'Stopped you?' Her eyes swelled out of the folds of crumpled skin. 'Who is this animal? My poor *vanuchka*.' Hastily wiping her hands on her apron, she clutched Valentina to her bosom, rocking her backwards and forwards. A distant rumbling, then a harsh crack of thunder shook the room seconds before the kitchen window filled with light.

'A typhoon,' she cried, releasing Valentina. Babushka only ever expected the worst. 'My

washing will be blown across the sea to Iceland!'
She darted outside.

Later, as they ate, Valentina asked her Mama.
'Do I look like a gipsy, a Russian gipsy?'

Madame dropped her fork. 'Who told you
this?'

'A guy at the theatre. I think he's the company's new choreographer.'

'Oh yes,' her eyes narrowed. 'I heard he's
somebody from London. What would he know
about gipsies?' A sudden thought occurred. 'Were
you flirting with him?' A second flash of sheet
lightning lit up the room. Everyone jumped.

'No, no, no. I hardly spoke ...'

'A choreographer from England. Pah! What
will he know of ballet? No great choreographers
have ever come from there, or musicians, or
composers ...'

'What about the Rolling Stones? Or East 17?'
Valentina interrupted, trying to lighten the
conversation.

She failed. 'You have no culture,' Mama thundered, stamping her fist on the table. 'Much as I
loathe and detest Russia, we had culture!'

'So why can't we stay longer while we're over
there? See the Winter Palace, go to St Petersburg?
Please, Mama?'

'I already explain.' Mama pushed her plate
away and lit a cigarette.

'You know what I want.' Tears sprang unbidden into Valentina's eyes. 'I so much want to find him, Mama. What harm can it do, after all these years?'

Babushka was wringing her hands and whispering in Russian.

'You will not talk of these things. Russia is over for us. You can never meet your father.' Her voice dropped and a new wheedling tone took over. 'You must hate me, Tina, to bring up this subject when you know what pain it gives me.'

'What about me? It hurts me too! It's like all my life something's been missing.'

'I've given you everything; nothing is missing!' Madame sprang to her feet and paced the floor, fitting a new cigarette into the holder with shaking hands. 'I expect you'd like to denounce me, your useless old mother. See me sent to Siberia!'

'I don't hate you,' Valentina told her, 'and anyway, they don't have the Gulag any more. We've just done Russia at school. It's all changed.'

'Don't tell me what it is like in my own country!' She glared at Valentina. 'I know Russia and I know Russian men. If it wasn't for you, I would never set foot in that country again.'

'Then why go to all this trouble? We could have taken the production to Prague, or New York, or London.'

'Because the Bolshoi is the best! And for you, my precious little Tina-lina-lina, only the best.' Her face softened. 'This opportunity is just the start. You will dance at the Bolshoi, and they all see you!'

Mama was working herself up into a state of

hysteria. She was exhausted from months of planning. It had been her energy that had driven the whole project. She had conceived and executed the most ambitious undertaking ever seen in Australian ballet – a student production of *Romeo and Juliet* to be performed in Russia. By single-mindedly taking on the Arts funding bodies and the State Dance Academy, Mama had done the impossible. Extra funds had been raised from large corporations. Madame Galliano was now a household word. Valentina and Ben appeared in magazines and TV talk shows. Interest in ballet was up, and bookings for all the companies had risen dramatically. Everyone marvelled at Madame's achievements.

Yet no one, not even Ben, knew why she was doing it. Only Valentina knew. It was to further Valentina's career, to leapfrog her into the limelight, so that she could be the international star her mother had failed to become.

'The most important thing is for you to concentrate. Drop all thees nonsense about your father. You have a great future ahead of you. You are going to be one of the greatest dancers in the world. Like Fonteyn ...'

Valentina was embarrassed. 'Margot Fonteyn was only average, until she met Nureyev.'

'Tina,' she begged, taking Valentina's hands and gazing up at her beseechingly, 'Promise me you will never marry a Russian. When you are much older, maybe twenty-four or -five, you could have a boyfriend ... perhaps someone like Ben, if he grows up and stops surfing. Or some other nice Aussie boy. And buy a nice house in a cul-de-sac. But until then, only the dance, okay?' There were real tears in her eyes. Valentina felt exhausted.

'Sure, mama,'

Madame's face lit up. 'Now I go to bed. Put everything away before you come.' She kissed the air, turned and swept out.

Babushka and Valentina stared at each other.

'Don't be too hard on your poor Mama,' she began. 'She loves you; she wants you to have the life that she was denied.'

'Who, who denied her?' She'd asked this question so many times she could recite the answer by heart. But it never rang true.

'You know, when we left Russia. And came here. She had to provide for us, buy this house, food. Teaching ballet is all she knew.'

'But she was still young, a great dancer; she could have joined the national company as a principal. Everyone says so.'

'You don't understand, she was downhearted. Our lives at home had been so ... difficult.'

Outside, rain drummed fitfully against the tin roof. Gusts of wind blew the bamboo so that it scratched the windows like tiny claws.

'Please tell me, Babushka; tell me about him. Why didn't he come with us?'

Her grandmother glanced up at the ceiling, as if her mama could hear. 'It's not my place to tell.'

'I'll be there next week. I'm going to try to find him. You know that. You might as well help. Please, please?'

Babushka's eyes clouded over. 'You mustn't. The past is history, best forgotten.'

A fresh surge of wind rattled the windows, knocking down the bunch of herbs her grandmother had hung up to dry on the ledge.

She looked so frightened, Valentina relented. There was no point in upsetting her further. There would be time once she reached Moscow, if she could get away from Mama, to do her own investigations. She stood up.

'Promise me you will not make trouble for your mama, when you go home?'

Valentina bent down and kissed her head. 'I can't promise, you know that. But I will be careful. Mama need never know.' Then she collected the dishes and took them over to the sink.

Picking up the fallen herbs, she breathed in their smell: thyme, oregano and rosemary. Rosemary for remembrance. It had been sixteen years since she last saw her father. All that lingered in her memory was his smell, something exotic, stronger than cologne. And his eyes, like chips of blue ice.

Gently she hung the rosemary back on the brass catch.

No, she could never forget him.

Surely he hadn't forgotten her?

# 2

Valentina made her way to morning classes as usual, picking her way over the palm fronds and debris drifting about after the storms. The street sweepers were grinding their way down Murray Street as she bought a takeaway coffee from Gino's and paused to read the headlines outside the newsagents. 'GIANT SWELLS – DEATHS AT SEA.'

'Thought you'd got rid of me?' Ben appeared out of the shop, his hair a tangle of wet, blond dreadlocks. He was munching a chocolate bar. 'Breakfast,' he added by way of explanation.

'Have you been home?'

'Na, waves were filthy. But I got a few hours sleep in the ute.' His hazel eyes sparkled. The smell of sea salt clung to his body, bare apart from a sleeveless T-shirt and faded board shorts.

'Take this.' Valentina handed over her polystyrene cup. 'Don't you think you ought to be preparing for the trip?'

'I am. Nothing prepares me better than catching a decent wave. I'm more amped now than if I'd had ten hours sleep.' And he looked it, his golden limbs loose and fluid. He tossed her bag into the back of the ute with his surfboard, and flung open the passenger door.

'How's my favourite grandma?' he asked as they took off. Ben always had a soft spot for Babushka.

'Fine, until I asked her if I looked like a Russian gipsy last night. She threw a wobbly, then Mama joined in and it was the usual *War and Peace* scene.'

Ben squealed out in front of a Mercedes, roared into third gear and overtook a bicycle. 'You know, you do look a bit like a gipsy – sort of wild and dangerous. No wonder Madame keeps you on a short leash.'

Valentina blushed. 'She only wants what's best for me.'

'Oh yeah? Fifteen-hour days and no remission for good behaviour?'

She was desperately trying to think up a flip remark that wouldn't make her sound like a mummy's girl, when the ute spluttered and ground to a halt.

'Damn. We've run out of petrol.'

'Don't you ever check anything?' Valentina

had no patience with Ben's casual approach. A perfectionist by nature, she never forgot anything.

'Walking's good for you, bossy-boots.' He flung open her door and grabbed her bag out of the back of the ute.

They set off in the early morning sun. The streets and gardens had been washed clean by the rains. Steam curled like liquid oxygen off the red tiled roofs.

It was always fun to be with Ben. They'd known each other since they were children. He had been a naughty nine-year-old, too big for his age and hyperactive. In desperation, his mother had brought him along with his sisters to Madame Laputin's school, hoping he'd learn some discipline. But to everyone's surprise he loved the music, loved the dancing. He had a natural understanding of his body and a perfect sense of balance. When the other kids at school teased him, he laughed along with their jokes and kept on going to ballet anyway. By the time he was a teenager, most of his friends accepted his 'hobby'.

The only real threat to his devotion to ballet came from surfing. The first time he stood up on a board was a revelation. He became addicted to the power of the ocean. Like thousands of other kids, he lived to surf, but unlike other kids his ballet training gave him mastery over his body. He became seriously good very quickly. The promoters moved in and offered him trips to Hawaii and Japan. But Ben was a traditional surfer. It was the silence of the sea and the spiritual sense of freedom he craved. Competitions didn't interest him and in any case, he was sure of his future. He wanted to dance.

'After today I'm going on a strictly macro-biotic diet,' he was saying. 'No more red meat, coffee, or milk products. Carrie's drawing up a diet sheet.' His twin sister Carrie danced in the student *corps-de-ballet*. She was a good dancer, but ballet came second in her life. Love came first.

They neared the gates of the Academy. Music from Chopin sweetened the air; the class pianist was warming up. They quickened their footsteps.

'Hey, will you be seeing any family in Russia while we're there?'

'I don't know. You know Mama; we'll be lucky if we get time out to eat. Anyway, the past is such a big secret with her. I don't even know where I was born!'

'And your father?'

'We'll only be there for a few days. I'll try, but there probably won't be enough . . . '

'We could track him down, if you set your mind to it. Stage One is for you to stand up to your mother.' He turned her round to face him. 'She has no right to keep you from meeting him. You do everything else she wants. Isn't it time you did something for yourself?'

Valentina hated hearing him criticise her mother. It was her relationship and if he couldn't understand it, that was his problem.

'Get lost, Ben. See you in class.' She dashed off to the changing rooms, her heart beating double-time. No one knew how hard Mama worked for her, or what she'd sacrificed. The least she could do was respect her wishes – or at least appear to. But the burning desire to see her father would be too strong once she got to Russia, she knew that.

This morning's teacher was as an elderly Hungarian whose supple movements gave no sign of his real age. He was a hard master, but after Madame, everyone was easy. Valentina took her place at the bar, rising and falling on her toes, watching herself anxiously in the mirror. She was her own worst critic, never satisfied, always striving for an elusive ideal of perfection.

'You have a beautiful smile, Valentina.' The master beamed kindly at her. 'The audience would like to see it.'

She mentally added 'smile and relax' to the list of instructions she carried in her head.

Five minutes later Ben joined her. The master frowned and shook his head as the music played on, pulling them into the hypnotic ritual of *pliés*, extensions, back bends and *enchainements*. Valentina tried to smile.

It was during a break for water, mid-morning, that the call came through for Ben and Valentina to see the Director in his office immediately.

'He wants to tell me I've won the gold medal for the year,' Ben suggested as they hurried towards the administration block.

'Dream on.'

'Okay, he's changed his mind about casting, and he's giving Juliet to the gorgeous redhead who came in from Western Australia.'

'You wish. More like re-casting Romeo – someone who gets to class on time?'

They turned the corner to find Madame Galliano lighting a cigarette, a pinwheel straw hat perched like a satellite dish on her head. 'Darlings,' she began as the Director emerged from his office.

'Ah, all three at once. Madame,' he gushed, gallantly taking her hand and bending to kiss it. Madame always presented her hand so that men had no other option but to bow. Then, turning to Ben and Valentina, he said, 'Sorry to disturb your class, but we have a change of plans. Come in.'

The Academy taught all the Arts, not just dance, and his office was a riot of paintings, posters, sculptures and strange musical instruments. A pot of coffee burbled behind a life-size *papier maché* naked woman. 'Anyone?' he offered.

Ben grinned, 'Yes please!'

'You're giving it up,' Valentina hissed.

Madame concentrated on removing a speck of ash from her mini-skirt. 'What have I left important rehearsals to hear?' she demanded.

The Director held up a fax. 'This has just come from Moscow, from the People's Art Bureau. There's been a mix-up. Apparently the Bolshoi is hosting the New York Ballet the week you were due to play *Romeo*.'

Madame dropped her cigarette holder and choked.

'Wait.' He held up his arm anxiously, as if to ward off an attack from Madame. 'All is not lost. It seems they have arranged to bring you forward. I've made some enquiries,' he hurried on, seeing the look on her face. 'I can get you all on flights from tomorrow onwards, more or less arriving in time to start dress and technical rehearsals on the Wednesday. You're opening Friday.'

Madame found her voice. 'This is preposterous. How can we possibly lose so much rehearsal time!' Her voice moved rapidly up the scales like a strangled cat. 'It is a plot. My enemies are out to ruin me; they want to see us fail!'

'No,' the Director answered firmly. 'I am sure it was simply inefficiency. They've had so many changes of staff over there – no one knows what they are doing any more.'

'They know what they are doing, believe me,' Madame shrieked. 'They are killing me!'

The Director looked despairingly at Valentina.

'We can be ready to leave in time,' she implored her mother. 'Ben and I are well rehearsed; we can go ahead and organise everything for the rest of you. And the production is almost ready now – you said so yourself.'

'But I cannot leave until next week,' she wailed. 'How can you manage without me? Your Russian is terrible!'

'Thanks! Look, I'll manage. We have no other choice.'

'Madame Galliano, even your superhuman efforts cannot change the fact that we are only a student production from Australia. How can we take precedence over the New York ballet?' The Director gazed out reasonably from behind bottle-thick glasses. 'And besides, I watched our principals yesterday; they were magnificent. Valentina, your Juliet was heart-breaking. I have never seen such a Juliet.'

Madame melted. 'You are right. Sometimes we can over-rehearse. The freshness is there. Are you sure you feel ready?'

Valentina wasn't sure. Her mind was whirling with conflicting emotions. If they left early without Mama, it would give her time alone to begin the search. On the other hand, she desperately wanted more time to work on Act Two. Oh, God! What a choice. They either went early, or gave up on the project altogether.

'We're ready.' She glanced over at Ben, who was gazing peacefully out of the window.

Ben had been wondering where he might have left his leg-rope when he realised everyone was looking at him expectantly. He said, 'I agree with Valentina.'

'Well, that's settled then,' said the Director, fishing around for the new itinerary. 'Here it is. Three seats on British Air tomorrow, change in London and Aeroflot to Moscow. The rest leave on

Tuesday. We took whatever we could. And I have to confirm them now.' He looked up quizzically.

Madame heaved a massive, long-suffering sigh. 'Okay, we take them.' Then, standing up, she said 'I'll see you at lunchtime, at the Theatre.'

It was after twelve when Valentina and Carrie met up at the theatre. Blonde like Ben, Carrie was wearing a batik shirt knotted above the navel, a long, flowing hippie-style skirt, and bare feet. She had rings in her ears, rings in her nose – even one in her nipple. Carrie was seriously into New Age philosophy.

They sat with the rest of the *corps-de-ballet*, watching the new choreographer finish morning class with the State dancers.

'Isn't he brilliant?' she whispered to Valentina.

'No. He's weird,' Valentina replied. She told Carrie about her encounter of yesterday. 'I was so glad Ben came along when he did.'

'He must have known you in a past life,' Carrie whispered seriously.

Valentina tugged her knee around her hip to loosen the pelvis. The choreographer was demonstrating the difficult *tour en l'air*, a double turn executed in mid-air. He was a bulky man and his landings lacked the soft catfall Ben could manage so easily. Yet he was magnificent to watch, leaping far higher than any of the other men in the ensemble.

24

'God, I hope not. Look at him showing off!'

'Maybe he was your husband in a past life and you were unfaithful to him and now he wants to get you in his thrall and punish you.'

Valentina raised an eyebrow. 'Have you been smoking something? Or reading Mills & Boon? Or both together?'

'No way! Not since the colonic irrigation. I'm pure and clean now, like Cliff Richard.'

'Which is more than I can say for him,' Valentina whispered as the dancers filed past them out of the studio. The man, wet with perspiration, strode past, glancing at her downcast face.

'Heavy! Bet he's a Scorpio,' Carrie pulled out a packet of dried seaweed and started nibbling. 'So what's your mother angry about now?'

Valentina told her about the change of plans.

'Will you and Ben go first?'

'Probably, since I speak a bit of Russian; and it wouldn't be safe on my own. The only person Mama would trust me with is Ben. Guess what?' She lowered her voice conspiratorially. 'Last night she actually said she might allow me to go out with a boy, as long as it's Ben, and as long as it's not until I'm twenty-five.'

'Big concession,' Carrie agreed. Then she added dreamily, 'I wish I could come with you.' She wondered what it would be like to be swept off her feet by a gorgeous Russian.

'I'll ask Mama.' Privately she thought her mother wouldn't allow a *corps-de-ballet* dancer out until the last minute. But it would be great to have Carrie for a few days. Valentina never spent time with friends. It would be like a holiday.

'Now, we begin!' Madame made her entrance as the imperious mistress of her own company. Most of the dancers were no longer her students, like Ben and Valentina, since they'd moved on to the Academy. But she'd trained them all and they were hers! With a great deal of dramatic gesturing, she outlined the problems and solutions, then dismissed them with the promise to post travel details later. Sweeping out, she ordered Valentina to follow.

Back in Madame's office, Valentina watched her swallow a handful of aspirins.

'You will go first, with Ben and one other; ask his sister. I'll manage the rest from this end, but you leave tomorrow morning, at six. There is so much to prepare. No rehearsals this afternoon; just go out and buy some warm clothing. It will be cold in Moscow. We can go over the rest of the details tonight. And Tina-lina?'

'Yes, Mama?'

'Don't worry about the shopping. Babushka can manage on her own.' She smiled sweetly, dismissing her.

Valentina wandered out in a daze. The most surprising thing was the calm way Mama was handling this sudden change of plans. Who could have predicted it? One minute going to pieces over absolute trivia, the next cool and resourceful in the face of a crisis. She never failed to surprise Valentina.

Carrie was in the foyer with Ben. They sat cross-legged on the floor with their eyes closed; Ben seemed to be sleeping.

'It worked!' Carrie shrieked, jumping up and down as she heard the good news. 'I manifested it! While you were in there, I closed my eyes, visualised a pink balloon, wrote my request on it and let the balloon float away. And it worked!' She threw her arms around Valentina's neck, mad with joy.

'Was that a primal scream?' Ben rubbed his eyes and uncoiled his long legs. 'Or Madame calling us to rehearsal?'

'There won't be any more rehearsals, not for us anyway. We leave tomorrow at six. The next time we dance,' she laughed, 'we'll be on the stage of the Bolshoi Theatre!'

Ben pulled her into his arms and lifted her into the air, then back into his arms. 'Vally, that is totally raging!'

Valentina disappeared into his bear hug.


She reached home in the late afternoon, before her mother. The street was deserted. Sultry air, heavy with moisture, promised another storm and left a greasy film on her skin. Exhausted from a failed shopping expedition, she was gradually realising the scale of the task ahead. Thank heavens Ben would be with her.

'Babushka?' she yelled, throwing down her

bag of toiletries and new underwear and reaching for a glass of water. No answer. She found her in the bedroom, under a mound of blankets.

'No worries, is just a flu.' She smiled weakly at Valentina. 'The weather.' But her skin was as dry as parchment and her forehead felt warm.

'I'll get the doctor.'

While they waited for her to come, Valentina made her grandmother tea and warmed some potato soup, playing her favourite Chesnokov and talking.

'We have no choice but to leave tomorrow. Oh, Babushka, I'm so excited and frightened. After all these years. What will it be like?'

'It will be cold now.' Her faded eyes grew moist. 'There will be frost flowers on the window panes. The wind will claw at your face like a cat. Spring comes late in Moscow.' A sad smile spread across her face. 'It was April when I first saw your grandfather.'

Valentina sat on the floor, listening.

'He was eating kasha and sour-cabbage soup in the tea rooms off Yvshenko Bridge.'

'Did you think he was handsome?'

'Oh, yes.' Babushka remained silent for a moment, drifting in her memories.

'Ivan Pavrych! Do you still think of him?'

Her grandmother looked confused. 'Ivan . . . ? Oh yes, yes. Ivan Pavrych.' A sad smile warmed her face. 'All the time, *vanuchka*; all the time. When you love someone, they never leave you, even when they're dead.'

'I know. I think of my father all the time.'

Babushka focused on her grand-daughter and sighed again.

A car door clattered shut in their driveway. 'That's either Mama or the doctor,' Valentina said, scrambling to her feet and making for the kitchen. Through the window she could see her mother arguing loudly with their neighbour, his red cattle dog snapping and barking over the fence. She poured the soup and returned to her grandmother.

'It's Mama. She's fighting with Bruce again. Here, it's ready now; I'll feed you.'

Babushka struggled upright, her eyes strangely bright. 'I have something for you.' She held out a small box. 'Is a present. Take it with you.' Then, falling back against her pillows, she waved away the soup and clutched the blankets to her face as if hiding something.

'Are you okay?' Valentina glanced briefly at the box; there was something metallic rattling inside. She pushed it deep into her pocket.

Babushka stared at her as if seeing someone else. 'When you get to Moscow, I want you to go to the water meadows, by the Moskva River. There is a church there, beside the Cathedral of the Virgin of Smolensk. It is a small church, white stone, with only one cupola. We were married there, your grandfather and I, in 1935. I want you to take a photograph for me. He is buried in the cemetery outside the church. Put some flowers on his grave. Buy violets, spring violets.'

Valentina held up the soup bowl. 'Of course I will. Now you must eat something. Come.' She filled the spoon.

Babushka clutched the blankets more tightly. 'Is important, *vanuchka*. Look at the stone in the cemetery. You will see.'

From the front of the house a door banged and footsteps clattered towards them. Babushka relaxed, her eyes half closed, and opened her mouth like a child.

# 3

The flight to London took twenty-five hours. Valentina sat beside two bogans from Sydney who spent most of the trip competing to see who could get drunker. Carrie, on the other aisle, was deep in a book called *Reincarnation: I Want Another Turn*. Ben had been upgraded to first class because they'd over-booked economy, and was enjoying the attentions of breathless air hostesses who thought he was a pop star. He'd given his occupation as 'professional entertainer'.

Valentina drifted in and out of sleep, refused countless meals and tried to read the Intourist *Guide to Russia*. She found a picture of the cathedral Babushka talked of, but not the small church. The box Babushka gave her held a pair of silver hoop earrings – gipsy earrings. She slipped them on, but felt let down. Somehow she'd hoped Babushka would tell her where to go and how to find her father.

And there was another even more pressing problem to worry about. The performance itself. What if she let her mother down, here in the very place she herself had been so successful? She was almost overwhelmed by the importance of it all. Would she be able to give her best with so much pressure?

The bogan dropped his head on her shoulder and let out a long burp, followed by heavy nasal breathing. She could smell the alcohol. Easing her shoulder forward, she unhitched her belt and escaped to the back of the plane.

'You are going to London?' A soft-voiced steward smiled at her.

'Russia. Moscow.'

'It'll be freezing. I just got back from there myself,' he answered, reaching up for a tourist book from the shelf above the cocktail bar. 'It's a lot better since *glasnost*.' He showed her a picture. A street darkened with snow, stacked with massive granite buildings. Grim tenements with unpronounceable names. The caption read 'Housing, available to every worker'.

'Doesn't Lenin look severe?' she offered.

'Oh, I thought he was rather cute, but the rest of it! Not what you'd call cafe society!'

The steward flicked the pages. 'But look at this; I just love the old parts of Moscow.' He showed her a picture of the Kremlin, like a fairy-tale castle, and the Winter Palace, and the Bolshoi itself! Imagine – she would soon be on the same stage that Nijinsky and Pavlova had danced on. She was overcome with fear and joy.

Ben trooped down the aisle, beaming, as they finally touched down in Heathrow.

'I've just had five beautiful women swooning over me,' he grinned, pulling her bag out of the overhead locker. 'Pity your company wasn't so interesting.' The drunks had slumped sideways and passed out on top of each other.

'It's the effect I have on men.' Valentina unbuckled gratefully and escaped.

'I know.' Ben reached into her overhead locker, pulling down her bag. 'I have the same effect on women, only with me they don't need the alcohol.'

'Are you boasting again?' Carrie pushed forwards. 'Here, do something useful.' She thrust her bag at him and wriggled impatiently. 'This is *sooo* exciting!'

They trudged down the stairs into a bright London morning. There were two hours before their next flight on the Russian airline, Aeroflot. Just enough time for Carrie to drink a fennel-twig tea and buy some English magazines. She wanted to know if the horoscopes were different. Valentina and Ben phoned home to see if Babushka was feeling better.

By lunchtime, they were aboard the Russian plane, which was half empty and smelling of kerosene. It was also freezing.

'The crew don't notice the cold,' Ben whispered. 'They keep warm russian about.'

It was a pathetic joke but it cheered up Valentina, who was growing increasingly nervous. Her filofax bulged with scraps of paper, lists and instructions. She'd just settled to prioritise her 'To Do' list, when the captain announced that unfortunately they would be landing in Budapest. 'But is no problem,' he assured them. 'We book you on night train to Moscva. Is very comforting.'

'Very comforting for whom?' Carrie's hazel eyes widened in dismay. 'How can they do that, without warning?'

'A whole day wasted in Budapest!' Valentina wailed, anxious to attack the problems. There was accommodation to find for twenty-three people, within budget. She had to see the Artistic Director of the Bolshoi to book a rehearsal studio and times. Then props, sets and publicity, all with only her half-forgotten smattering of Russian.

'I think it's great.' Ben pushed back his hair, now washed free of dreadlocks and falling like corn-coloured silk over his face. 'We deserve a day off to enjoy ourselves. Lighten up, Val; remember having a good time?'

'But we have no street maps; we don't know the place. What will we do?' she wailed.

'My horoscope says *Romance is highlighted*,' Carrie read from a magazine she'd picked up at Heathrow. 'Let's just be open. Everything happens for a reason.'

Out of the window they could see Budapest lurching below them. It was arranged haphazardly on either side of the river, and the Danube shone as blue as a sailor's coat.

'Let's find the train station before we do anything else. Then we can dump the bags and double-check those train seats are booked. After this, I don't trust anybody.' Valentina buckled on her safety belt for landing.

'I vote we just cut loose and rage,' answered Ben, to tease Valentina.

Budapest Airport was chaos and everything was written in Hungarian, but they found the train station and left their luggage, thanks to Ben's talent for miming. Then Carrie insisted they 'go with the flow', which in practice meant following the hunk in the soldier's uniform. Fortunately he headed into the city centre with the other commuters on an underground metro.

The air was sharp, but the mid-morning sun, warm and buttery, lit up the city. Bronze Gothic buildings crouched beneath rocky outcrops on the other side of the Danube. They'd never seen anything like it in Australia. The train rattled past the rock walls and housing, then dived suddenly underground for a few stops, before swooping back up into the sunlight. They passed parks full of daffodils bursting through emerald grass and medieval houses huddled together for warmth.

'Like the Big Dipper!' Valentina was entranced. She was beginning to relax. 'See, I'm having fun,' she said defiantly to Ben who looked disbelieving.

When they reached Grand Central Station they melted into the crowds pouring out into a sophisticated street. It was filled with smart shops and street cafés. They saw elegant old men wearing gloves and carrying silver-topped walking sticks. There were fashionable ladies in hats, and violinists on every street corner. The air was perfumed with coffee, smoked sausages and sugared pastry. Excitement was contagious.

'Let's eat!' The street smells were too much for Ben. He pushed open the door of a tiny brasserie, warmed by an open fire, and pointed at an amazing display of food in a glass cabinet.

'I'm freezing.' Valentina stretched her fingers out to the fire, 'I never managed to find a coat, or sweaters and things.'

'And I haven't shopped for ages. Why don't we?' Carrie punched her brother on the arm. 'Without him. He only complains.'

'Wouldn't dream of cramping your style,' Ben agreed as a steaming pile of Gundel *crèpes* arrived, smothered in chocolate sauce and stuffed with almond and raisin paste.

'Mama would kill us. I haven't had dessert since I was ten!' Valentina was shocked at how easy it was to break her food rules in a foreign country.

'I won't tell if you don't.' Carrie filled her mouth. 'This is so sinful. And I don't care.'

It was almost an hour later when the girls staggered out into the street looking for clothes shops.

'Over there.' Carrie pointed to a boutique. A severely elegant sweater on a stylish model was the only garment in the window.

'Too expensive!' Valentina had her Visa card, but she rarely used it. She'd bought nothing for the trip except a few toiletries and warm underwear. Having no confidence when it came to buying clothes, and nowhere to wear them, she'd always lived in tracksuits and warm-up gear. She stared at the wine-red cashmere sweater. 'I can't imagine myself in anything like that.'

'Why not?' Carrie gripped her by the elbow and propelled her into the shop.

The next thing she knew she was staring at her reflection and asking the round-faced assistant to write down the price. The piece of paper she held up was covered in zero's.

'But I can't; it's thousands of something.'

'So what? You look great and it'll make you feel great. That's all that counts.'

Valentina's hair fanned out over her shoulders, black velvet on crimson. If it had been anyone else she would have raved about it. But on her? The cashmere felt as soft as a new-born kitten as she ran her hands down her sides. Slim fitting and short, it emphasised her tiny waist and high breasts. 'I look too sophisticated. It isn't my style.'

'Yes, it is a bit capitalist yuppie.' Carrie was pushing buttons on her calculator, doubtfully. 'On the other hand, good grief! It's only twenty-five dollars. For cashmere!'

Once they'd discovered the exchange rate was in their favour and clothes so cheap, a strange madness took over. Valentina, who'd never bought a garment in her life without her mother's approval, ended up with a camel coat, two sweaters, gloves, exquisite fur-lined, high-heeled boots, her first-ever mini-skirt, a pull-on woollen hat that made her face look like a pixie, and a short satin nightdress with French lace. The nightdress was an act of madness. A whole year's savings had been blown in one mad spree.

Carrie, who had begun by swearing she would only buy a simple cashmere shawl and woollen socks for yoga, ended up with a billowing woollen coat and cape, with hat and boots to match. With her height and dancer's grace, she looked like a model on the catwalk.

'I feel like Claudia Schiffer,' she sighed, preening at her reflection in the window of a coffee shop, 'and it's time for a caffeine hit.' She pushed open the door and collapsed on a blue velvet seat surrounded by carrier bags.

Valentina was starting to feel guilty. 'Mama will hate the sweater. It's too tight. And the boots are too sexy. And as for the nightdress!'

'She can talk! She'll just be nervous of the competition. Anyway, you can't meet your father dressed like a schoolgirl.'

'Why not? After all, I've been living with

schoolgirlish fantasies all my life. Like finding lost fathers in countries as big as Russia in three days, without so much as a name to start off with.'

'Put like that, it does sound a bit daunting. But if it's meant to be, it'll happen. Now, I'm wasting good eating time. When do we meet Ben?'

'He said something about going water-skiing this afternoon, and we have to go straight to the station to meet him at six.'

'There's time.' She ordered steaming bowls of *gulyas* thick with beef, potato, sour cream and paprika.

Valentina cheered up. 'Isn't this all the wickedest fun!' Her eyes glittered like polished ebony buttons. Cheeks, pink from the cold, shone against the deep-red sweater. 'I thought you didn't eat meat,' she added, ripping off a crust of bread and dipping it cheerfully into her soup.

'It's my splurge day and a holiday. That means I can eat four times as much as normal,' Carrie grinned. 'Anyway, I don't have any solos, I can afford to eat a little more than you. Don't you make me feel guilty; that's one of Madame's tricks.'

'What do you mean?' Valentina looked up sharply.

Carrie levelled her gaze, then shrugged. 'Forget it. Oh, look!'

A trumpet flourish caught their attention. Outside, in the square, a crowd had begun to gather. Lively gipsy music, violins and accordions, rose above the polite chatter in the restaurant.

'Is a folk festival,' the waitress explained. 'He comes from everywheres, the peoples, to dance and sing. From Russia, Czechoslovakia, Romania, everywheres. Stay, see!' she instructed, proud of her English. 'You Americans!'

They peered through the steamed-up window at the spectacle outside. Dancers in national costume took turns on the small, makeshift stage. Crowds gathered, clapping and stamping, swaying to the music, all smiles and colour and bright ribbons.

'If only our audiences reacted like that.' Valentina's eyes shone. 'See how involved they are? I adore ballet, I feel the music intensely when I dance, but I've never seen audiences so excited by ballet.'

'That's because classical ballet is controlled. It's all technique and form. That kind of folk dance,' Carrie waved her bread, 'is raw, unadulterated emotion. That's why you're so brilliant, Val. You've got control. I wish I had,' she moaned, ordering another bowl of *gulyas*.

A new group took the stage. There were only four of them, one man and three women. Valentina sat up. She could tell by the way they held themselves, beautifully poised, waiting for their music, that they were trained classical dancers.

'Excuse me, I think I'd like to get a closer look. Be back soon,' and she slipped out into the street.

The cold stung her cheeks and she hugged herself, staring at the lead dancer. He was performing a magnificent solo, a proud, foot-stamping display of sheer machismo. The violin parried with him, like a duet, and they teased each other, building up the momentum slowly and seductively. He was tall, young, blond, about twenty, with heavily muscled thighs and calves. The way he held the turns, the speed he built up on such a small stage, made him undoubtedly a professional. Next he pulled one of the women into his arms, twirling her round faster and faster. The audience loved it, clapping approval, stamping feet, shouting encouragement. Then he called another to join him, then another. He stood alone at the vortex of the dancers, while they spun around him, a blur of colours. But it was the expression on his face which held Valentina – powerful and uncompromisingly masculine. Not like the boys she knew.

She thought of Ben and his lazy, lopsided grin and the boys at the Academy with their non-committal, put-down humour and cool boredom. There was nothing non-committal about this guy. He was fire and ice, his body hot with movement, his eyes like cold sapphires.

Now she was sure he was staring at her. She could feel the heat of it warm her body. Her cheeks burned. The dance was reaching a crescendo, the crowds roaring and stamping in time with the drums. Other dancers were joining him on the stage, making it hard for her to see him – just flashes of his golden, sun-lit hair flicking hard on the turns, his eyes smiling now, teeth a white blur. He was controlling the dancers and the audience as effortlessly as his own body, like a sun-god.

Then – silence! The dancers froze, arms held high, faces triumphant.

Suddenly the audience erupted. Valentina yelled with excitement, cheering wildly along with the mob. And as they pushed forward, arms outstretched to shake hands with the dancers, she found herself pressed against the wooden boards, looking straight into his dazzling blue eyes. Her stomach churned. She caught her breath sharply.

'*Ya tebya uravlous?*' He reached out his hand to her, smiling.

Russian! Confused, unable to understand the words, she guessed he wanted to know if she liked the dance. She answered, '*Zdorovo!*'

'Americano?'

Obviously her Russian left a lot to be desired.

Just then, a fat middle-aged woman, bundled into several overcoats, pushed her aside to grab the dancer with both hands and Valentina lost sight of him. But she didn't lose the image of his eyes, burning into hers.

Disturbed, she turned back to the restaurant. She stumbled out to the toilets. In the mirror she could see her cheeks, pink as petunias. *Oh God, it's happened to me again*, she breathed. She'd felt like this before, more than a year ago, when she was seventeen.

42

A visiting tutor from the Strasbourg Ballet had spent six weeks at their Dance School, working with her mother. He'd been almost twice her age, but when he danced, she melted. Once, he demonstrated a *pas-de-deux* from *Les Sylphides* with her, and she became so excited she couldn't sleep for weeks. When Mama noticed what had happened, she sent the tutor home. The poor guy probably didn't even know why. It took her several months to recover from the shock of physical attraction, and she vowed to stay away from men. Mama was right; they only distracted you and got in the way of your goals.

Drying off her face, she wandered back into the cafe. Through the plate-glass window she could see the dance troupe disappearing into a van. She watched as its dusty-blue bumper turned the corner – out of sight, and out of her life. Suddenly feeling tearful, she did what she always did when strong feelings unbalanced her; she fixed a bright smile on her face and straightened her shoulders.

'I want to go sightseeing,' she announced, changing the subject to stop Carrie staring at her so curiously.

So they spent the rest of the afternoon wandering round the haphazard alleys and squares of old Budapest. She loved the medieval churches and the over-decorated houses reaching out to each other over the cobbled streets.

'I feel like Cinderella,' Carrie said, admiring her new outfit in a shop window. 'As if any minute now a golden coach will clatter round the corner, pulled by white horses with scarlet plumes. This place is like being in Disneyland, but for real.'

'Isn't this where Dracula was filmed?' Valentina wondered, trying to put herself off the dancer by picturing him with werewolf fangs.

Like children let out of school for a day, they roamed the magical streets of Budapest. Several times they crossed the Danube, exploring until the sun dipped in the sky and it was time to find the train station.

'I wonder how Ben spent his day,' mused Carrie, sitting back exhausted on her seat on the Metro as it flashed past churches, stations, factories, and apartment blocks.

'I wonder where he is right now?' answered Valentina, thinking of someone else.

'At the train station, I hope. You looked a bit strange when you joined us in the coffee shop. Were you feeling sick?'

Valentina thought of telling Carrie about *him*, then decided it would sound ridiculous. Falling for a fleeting image, a dancer in a street show!

Instead she said, 'I feel terrific. This has been the best day of my life. I adore Budapest. The shopping was such fun, and eating whatever we liked, going wherever we wanted.' She leaned forward gripping Carrie's hands, eyes shining. 'Wasn't it fantastic?'

Carrie looked troubled. 'Haven't you spent a whole day playing before?'

Valentina had to think. 'When I was younger, maybe. When we all used to go down to the Harbour, remember? Since High School, all I've ever done is work.'

'Every day?'

'Mama built a *barre* in the sitting room and put up mirrors so I could practise on Sundays and public holidays. And anyway, I had to catch up with school work at the weekends. I spent so much time dancing, there was no time for holidays.'

Carrie looked horrified. 'Your mother should be reported to the Society for the Prevention of Cruelty to Children.'

She laughed. 'It isn't like that. She does it for me; she knows I want to be a great dancer.'

'Yes, but why?'

Valentina shifted in her seat. It was so uncomfortable. 'Every one of us wants to be the best we can. Don't you?'

'I dance because I love it, like those gipsies today. Why do you dance?'

The train suddenly blacked out as it rushed underground. The wind whistled past their faces, drowning her reply. Then they emerged into the bustle of Budapest Station at dusk, lit by the strange magenta light of the dying sun. There was a general scramble for bags, as they found themselves surrounded by crowds of commuters, soldiers, families with babies wrapped up like balloons, and hucksters selling cigarettes, kebab sticks, boiled water and vodka. A band played

Tchaikovsky with brass instruments and a vast, ornate clock tolled six bells.

'It's Thelma and Louise!' Ben suddenly appeared from the crowd. His tangled hair poked out from under a black knitted beanie, his broad shoulders were hunched inside a checked Quicksilver jacket, and his frozen hands were stuffed into his jeans pockets – like a surfie at North Narrabeen. He was so dear and familiar, both girls dropped their bags and hugged him.

Grinning with pleasure, he handed them their tickets. 'Been here for an hour. The bags are stashed on the train, and you have the pleasure of sharing a sleeping compartment with me!'

By six-thirty they were pulling out of the station, away from the sunset, heading east into the vast dark hinterland that was Russia. Valentina watched the lights of the station fade.

'You look hot in that new sweater,' said Ben, joining her in the corridor. He'd taken off all his jackets and sweaters and was down to his usual T-shirt and board shorts. 'And I'm just hot.' He pulled down the window an inch, pressing his face to the gap to catch the icy air whistling in.

'Is Moscow in the tropics or are they cremating us in here?' Ben had never been known to feel the cold. 'You both look great,' he added kindly, running his hand down Valentina's back. 'I love fluffy sweaters; it's like stroking the cat. Will you be curling up at the foot of my bed tonight?'

'You wish. I want to stay here and think.' She pushed him gently away. Ben was such a puppy dog sometimes, playful and sweet; but she wanted to be alone.

'Well, I'm off. I'm exhausted with the water skiing. My arms are ripped out of their sockets. See ya.' He slid open the door to their sleeping compartment. She could see gas lamps on either side of the double bunks spreading a ghostly yellow light; midnight-blue blankets dark against the white cotton sheets; the unwanted fourth bunk heaped up with bags and books.

'Don't peek when we come to bed.' Valentina gave him a quick hug and turned back to her window. The train was gathering speed, hurtling past blackened farmyards and orchards silhouetted against the pearly dusk. Somewhere down the west end of the train, a violin wailed. A sad song. She couldn't sleep just yet.

Suddenly, at the end of the east-bound corridor, a noise erupted. Light and music spilled out of the sliding door. Carrie came charging towards her, a crimson paisley scarf flung over her shoulder, hair flying wildly around her face.

'Valentina, come and join us, we're having a brilliant time. Guess who I've just met?' Over her shoulder a group of dancers in gipsy costumes trooped after her.

Valentina didn't feel like partying. 'Thanks, but I'd rather be alone for a while.' The folk dancers crowded around her, smiling encouragement, chattering in Russian.

Carrie grabbed her hand, dragging her back towards the music. 'Never refuse an experience,' she announced, shoving back the door. Several carriages later, Valentina found herself in a brightly-lit saloon car with a bar at one end and black leather banquette seats along the windows. Music blared out from a radio – Russian dance music. A man was twirling low, in the traditional Georgian cossack dance, kicking his legs out straight with enormous strength. Around him people were laughing, drinking beer, yelling and clapping. The temperature, already too hot in the other compartments, was like a sauna in here. Valentina brushed her hair back and escaped to the opposite end of the saloon, where she could see an empty seat by the window.

'You didn't tell me you were Afstrylyan?'

She looked up startled, into the same blue eyes that had haunted her all day. Not knowing whether to scream in terror or fall into his arms, she was saved the choice.

Her legs collapsed under her and she fell into the chair.

**4**

From the other end of the compartment Valentina could see Carrie giggling and tossing her blonde head. She was surrounded by young men drinking beer from small brown bottles marked 'Pivo'. The barman, a red-haired bull of a man, squeezed himself up and down the tiny bar, clanking bottles and wrenching off tops. They hissed softly, almost drowned out by the merriment.

The young man stood in front of her.

He was watching patiently, *waiting for her to do something*. His hair shone in the gas lamps like a blazing golden halo. His eyes were the purest blue she'd ever seen, the blue of Delft china or star sapphires.

She was in a turmoil. Looking down, she became aware that her new black velvet skirt was far too short. Almost the entire length of her thigh, clad in black tights, was exposed. But if she tugged it now, he would think her self-conscious. Even her breasts, prominent in the ruby-red sweater, suddenly seemed like an invitation. Heat flushed through her body, tingling her scalp and burning her cheeks. She looked up through her lashes, motioning him to sit.

'I saw you today. You were watching the dance. Yes?'

She nodded, not trusting her voice.

'And now you are here. Is coincidence.' He stared at her intently, his arm loose against the back of the chair, legs splayed nonchalantly. 'What you do here, on train to Muscva?'

'I'm with a group.' She glanced over at Carrie to reassure herself, but the young men formed a wall round her. They circled, stamping and clapping and chanting. 'The blonde girl over there ... and I ... and others, we're dancers ...'

'Ah, so you were watching me like a critic?' He leaned forward, an eager smile curving his wide sensual mouth. 'And what did you think?'

'I thought you were magnificent.' They were not the words she meant to say, but they slipped out before she could stop them.

He sat back satisfied. 'So. We see each other in Budapest, now we meet in train, and we are in the same profession. Is too many coincidences. Is Fate.'

A sudden roar of noise erupted from the circle of men. They parted to reveal Carrie twirling in the centre like a dervish, arms high, cape swirling and an ecstatic smile on her face.

**50**

'Your friend dances well. Show me how you move,' he commanded, taking her hand and pulling her upright. The ancient battered stereo played balalaika music, but it was barely audible above the cheerful racket. 'My name is Alexei,' he began, taking both her hands and raising them, stepping sideways and bending at the knee as she'd seen the gipsy dancers do in Budapest. 'Follow me!'

Valentina desperately wished she was wearing jeans or a loose skirt. But she pulled up her mini a fraction, and fell into the rhythm of the dance, dipping and turning around Alexei. He was facing her, holding her with his eyes as the music speeded up. A couple of people drifted closer, clapping time. At each fourth step, he changed direction, flicking his head and motioning her to follow with his eyes. Then he introduced a new step, then another and another, until she felt dizzy with concentrating. Her hair whisked across her face or flew out behind her in the turns. And all the time his eyes, like blue spheres of ice, held her mesmerised. The energy from his hands melted down her arms, relaxing her, as she gave way to the music and the dance. Her body and Alexei's were no more than instruments of the music, swaying and circling at its command.

They ended with a flourish, spinning and collapsing at the same time onto the banquette seat. Valentina burst out laughing with pleasure, giddy with the strangeness and excitement of it all. Nor did it seem unusual when he handed her one of the ice cold bottles of beer. Drinking beer and laughing with a ravishingly handsome stranger, while rushing through the black night towards Russia, seemed perfectly normal.

In fact, it was perfect.

Later, she excused herself and went to the toilet cubicle to cool her face with dampened tissue. The face in the mirror was an exotic stranger, nothing like Valentina Galliano from Brisbane, Australia. She peered at her reflection. Brilliant coal-black eyes, flushed cheeks, triumphant smile. *He likes you*, she whispered, *and why shouldn't he? You look stunning and you're free. There's nothing to stop you getting to know him better. Except*, she turned away miserably, scrunching up the tissue, *the fact that he's probably just amusing himself on the train. Why would he be interested in me? After tomorrow we'll never see each other again. And anyway, I've got enough to deal with as it is.* She hurled the tissue into the bin.

Someone banged the door. 'Are you in there?' Carrie yelled.

Valentina flung it open.

'I was getting worried about you.' Carrie stood swaying in the tiny corridor outside. She looked tired.

'Isn't this exciting,' breathed Valentina. 'I'm so glad you came to get me.'

'The bar's closed and those mad dancers want to open a bottle of vodka for us in their compartment.' Carrie stifled a yawn. 'I can think of nothing worse than being cooped up in a stuffy compartment with a bunch of drunk, horny Hungarians, unless they all looked like the one you were dancing with. Are you hooking in to him?'

'No!' Valentina hated that expression. 'I'm just talking to him. They're not Hungarians, they're Russians, and I was practising my Russian. Those guys are students like us. They go to the same Academy my mother went to in Kirov. I was just interested, that's all. Don't look at me like that.'

'So you don't fancy him?'

'Why should I?' she lied. 'We're only passing strangers on a train; we'll never see him again. Bit stupid to start fancying him, isn't it?'

'Love usually is stupid,' Carrie sighed. 'I do admire you. How do you manage to stay sensible in the face of such fantastic temptation?'

'Discipline and Obedience!' laughed Valentina, imitating her mother. 'But I'm not ready for bed yet. What say we pop in, just for a few minutes. Come on, Carrie, never refuse an experience. Remember?'

Carrie stared at her. 'This doesn't sound like you. Have you been drinking?'

'I've had one bottle of beer, and I couldn't finish it, it tasted of cat pee,' she answered truthfully. 'But I know how boring it'll be tomorrow with nothing to do but count the collective farms. We might as well stay up late tonight.'

'Oh dear,' Carrie sighed dramatically, 'Valentina Unchained! Who would have thought there was a party animal under that cool exterior? Well, I'd better not leave you; Brad Pittski may be too much for you to handle.' She turned wearily back to the bar. 'In fact, you'd better leave him to me,' she grinned wickedly. 'Ben would never forgive me if anything happened to you.'

Their new friends waited for them in the corridor outside their compartments. Alexei took Valentina's hand with an air of ownership and led her in. It was already filled with people from the troupe. Smoke billowed, camouflaging their faces, soft in the lamplight. A samovar bubbled in the corner and rows of small tea glasses in copper holders lined the wall. A competition was being held to see who could mix the best drink. The ingredients included tea, vodka, apple juice and a mystery green liquid. Loud roars of disapproval greeted every mix which was handed round to taste, before the next guy took his turn, slopping and spilling the bottles.

Valentina watched Carrie accept a tea glass of the mixture and swallow it. Alexei held up his hand to refuse the glass for her.

'Is rubbish,' he decided. 'No good for you.' He nodded at two people sprawled on the top bunk playing cards, and they dutifully scrambled down and hurried out into the corridor. Alexei helped Valentina into their place. It was a tight fit. The only way she could get comfortable without taking off her skirt was to lie sideways, facing him.

She watched him strip off his cotton jacket and

boots. He curled up barefoot like a cat in the small space left, wearing only a white singlet and soft drawstring pants. Taking out a small bottle of vodka, he poured two tooth glasses and handed her one, saying '*Glasnost!*' and draining his glass. Valentina couldn't take her eyes off his face. It was quick, mobile, expressive of every emotion. Right now it was warm with pleasure. He joined in the mixing contest enthusiastically from the top bunk, shouting encouragement and tasting the appalling mixtures. Occasionally he would glance sideways at her and flash a smile so beautiful, her heart almost stopped beating.

The heat in the crowded compartment was making it harder and harder for her to think clearly. After several scalding sips of vodka, she quietly lowered it down to Carrie, sitting underneath. But not before she'd felt its heat warm her body. Alexei, to make room for her to relax, had lifted her feet onto his lap and taken off her shoes. Now, he was absent-mindedly stroking her ankles and toes while shouting instructions down below. Eventually the mixing game gave way to a game of chess with four or five people on each side making drunken suggestions. The players themselves were almost incapable of moving the pieces and yelled back good naturedly.

Valentina felt she'd died and gone to heaven. She watched his profile, strong and mysterious in the gas light, speaking in the half-understood language of her childhood, the rhythm of the train rocking her like a baby. And his eyes. Something about that startling blue. It was the colour of a Russian summer sky, washed clean of smog and rain. She wanted to reach out and hold his restless, quicksilver body, almost naked beside her. He sat like a coiled spring, the muscles in his arms and chest silhouetted sharply every time he moved.

She felt her head grow heavy and lay down on the pillow so that she could watch him, soothed by the delicious sensations his fingers made softly trailing her feet. Her mother seemed a million miles away, in a different space and dimension. The performance, the responsibilities, her curiosity about her father – everything was fading into insignificance. There was only now.

'Wake up, Vally. We'd better get back to our compartment. These guys could go on all night.' Carrie intruded into her consciousness.

'I'm too comfortable to move,' she heard herself say. 'I'll be along in a minute.'

'I bring her.' Alexei held out his hand, introducing himself to Carrie. 'Alexei Ivanoff, Principal Dancer, Kirov Academy.'

Carrie wilted visibly, then whispered to Valentina, 'Oh, God, he's fantastic. Is there room up there for me?'

'It's not like that,' Valentina felt embarrassed. 'It's just the heat; I'm tired.'

'Whatever you reckon,' she grinned, adding, 'Good luck with him – and be careful. These guys are mad,' before slipping out of the door.

'You stay with me?' Alexei leaned over towards her.

'No. I mean yes, for a bit.' His eyes bored into hers, and his hand lay warm on her thigh.

'You have boyfriend in Afstrylya?'

'No. I'm too busy, I have no time.' If only she could stay forever here in this tiny magical space looking into Alexei's eyes, listening to the laughter, the balalaika, the music of her native tongue. He leaned forward again, stroking her hair away from her face.

'You remind me of a beautiful gipsy, the ones that come into Muscva every spring from Albania.'

'My mother trained at the Kirov, but I don't know where she was born. I don't know who my father is.' For the first time in her life she admitted this shameful fact. It had been easier in Australia just to say her father was in Russia. 'Perhaps he was a gipsy? My Babushka is from Moscow.'

Alexei ran his fingers over her lips and cheeks, gently tracing her eyebrows and eyes. 'Is possible. We have Albanians in our ensemble. They are strong and passionate,' his fingers fell to her shoulder, 'like you.' Then he raised her up towards him, kissing her with incredible gentleness, probing her lips and mouth with soft movements of his tongue. She could feel his hand stroking her back and side. Swooning, she struggled for breath as his hand soothed her breast as tenderly as a mother with a baby.

'No, Alexei.' She pulled away. Down below,

she could see the gang sucking bottles of vodka and arguing loudly. 'Not here. I . . . '

But it was too late, he turned away and poured another drink. 'Is no matter.' She noticed for the first time how perfect his hands were. Strong, masculine hands with the slightest dusting of gold hair. She wanted to stroke them.

'I'm sorry,' she murmured, sitting upright and resting her head against his shoulder. The strangeness of the opposite sex. After living all her life with her mother and grandmother, she could never work out how men thought. He talked now to his companions, the kiss forgotten. His voice, a thrilling deep baritone, resonated through her head as she pressed her ear to his shoulder. Jealous of losing his attention, she felt rejected, as if she'd failed him. Perhaps it would be better to go. She slipped down to the floor.

'Goodnight,' she whispered, sliding open the door and melting out into the night.

Theirs was one of the last carriages. Panting, she paused to collect herself outside the door. Someone, probably Ben, had left the sliding window in the corridor down a centimetre. The wind, sharp as a knife, howled to get in. Valentina took several cold breaths before opening the door quietly. A top bunk was empty, its little gas light still burning. Deep breathing filled the room. She undressed thankfully, turned off the light and climbed up into the warm cotton sheets.

The window blind was open and a ghostly

green pre-dawn light illuminated a landscape carved from ice. Rocking with the train, she stared at the cold curdled sky above a flat snowscape. She pictured Alexei dressed like a Hussar, charging across the white fields on a pure black stallion. Her hero.

Then she thought about his mouth, its surprising softness and heat. She hadn't known what it would be like to kiss a man. She'd wanted it to go on for ever, but then he'd touched her in a way that was too exciting and like a frightened child she'd pulled back. *What must he be thinking of me*? she wondered, squirming with embarrassment. How could she have been so uncool? She tried to calm her mind, filled as it was with a thousand wonderful images, smells, sights, sounds . . . and Alexei. Eventually she slept.


'Is it the Sleeping Beauty or Juliet?'

Ben stood in front of her, his eyes almost level with hers on the top bunk. She blinked into his bright topaz eyes.

'Or just a hangover?'

Valentina dragged out her pillow and threw it at him. 'You know I never drink!' The compartment was filled with bright white light. 'Where are we?'

'We're coming up to the Ukrainian border, I've just talked to a train guard. Carrie's gone to meditate in the guard's van, or so she said. She was wearing make-up and perfume – bit suss. What did you girls get up to last night?'

'We met some dancers from the Kirov Academy, and they showed us folk dances in the saloon bar. It was great.' Her eyes shone as she pushed herself upright. 'How do we get breakfast?' She ran her fingers through her hair, examining her reflection in the mirror above the bunk. The whites of her eyes had pink veins etched around the pupils. Cigarette smoke from last night.

'We don't. There are only the leftovers of the jam and buns I bought in Budapest. They don't have restaurant cars on Russian trains, just saloons. You would know about that,' he added nastily.

Valentina jumped down, enchanted by the silvery landscape floating past. She was not going to let Ben annoy her with his usual teasing. 'How exquisite! The snows still haven't melted. Maybe we'll see the Kremlin and the Bolshoi as I remember them, like fairytale castles covered in icing sugar.'

'I could do some snowboarding,' Ben joined in, pouring some tea from the samovar.

'No way. Surfing is one thing, you've done it for ever; but snowboarding's too dangerous. You can't afford any injuries. Promise me, Ben?' She accepted the steaming glass of tea and the red sticky bun he handed her.

'You can be so boring sometimes,' he sighed.

The train was slowing down and up ahead they could see a squad of serious-looking soldiers. With a final jerk and scrunching of metal it stopped to let them embark. They swarmed aboard, carrying Kalashnikov rifles and old-fashioned mobile phones.

'Thank heavens for border guards.' Ben looked interested. 'This is the first bit of excitement since we got on this train.'

Valentina jumped up to get dressed while Ben dashed off to investigate.

Presently he returned with a heavily armed soldier in camouflage.

'They want our documentation.' He wasn't looking quite so enthusiastic. Valentina neatly retrieved it from the orderly paperwork in her brief-case. She handed it over to the soldier.

'Ukraine visas?' asked the soldier. He had a mean, ferrety face.

'We're not visiting the Ukraine,' Ben answered. 'We had plane tickets to Moscow, and Aeroflot re-routed us. We have Russian visas,' he added hopefully.

'This is big problem. You are in the Ukraine now without visa.'

'But we're not getting off the train.'

'Is illegal.' The soldier stood his ground, his face implacable, the beady eyes flicking across at Valentina. 'Are you Valentina Galliano?'

'Yes.'

'Born in Moscow?' he squinted at her passport.

'Yes.'

'Come with me.' He held open the door and waited impassively for her. She pulled on her new boots and camel-haired coat.

'Hold on, mate. I'll come too.' Ben grabbed his jacket and squeezed her hand for reassurance, following her down the corridor and out of the train.

Valentina thought of all the terrible stories she'd heard about people vanishing in the night, bodies turning up in the woods, relatives disappearing in broad daylight, unexplained gunshots in the distance. 'Ben,' she whispered shakily, 'what do you think this is about?'

'It's a surprise party to welcome you back to the land of your birth. The other soldiers have gone ahead to blow up balloons and put on a keg.'

'I know what sort of "blowing up" guys like these do,' she hissed. But before he could reply, they were ushered onto the platform and into a tiny, frost-hardened building, reeking of oil from a solitary burner. Valentina shuddered with cold. A stiff-backed man in a sheepskin greatcoat sat on the only stool in the room, crowded round by soldiers.

'G'day,' Ben called out cheerfully, extending his hand to the man.

He gazed at Ben silently, his eyes both indifferent and concentrated at the same time. Everyone froze. Another soldier came in and handed him an envelope, muttering in his ear. The large man glanced inside, then stuffed it into an inside pocket. He carried on staring impassively at Ben and Valentina as if they were insects under a microscope.

Finally he barked in rapid Russian at the soldier who'd brought them in. A round of dutiful laughter greeted his joke.

'What'd he say?' Ben mouthed at her.

'I think he's asking if you're a deviant.'

Ben started to laugh, before Valentina kicked him surreptitiously on the ankle. He thought for a moment, his hands plunged deep in his pockets. Then, like a conjurer, he pulled out a pair of reflective Raybans with a lime-fluoro strap. Stepping forward, he handed them to the officer in charge as gravely as if they were the crown jewels.

The officer put them on gingerly, lacing them over his head so that Valentina could see her frightened reflection in his eyes. The bright green strap shone like neon lighting in the dim room. Ben clapped his hands in delight at the ludicrous sight. One of the soldiers joined in, then another and another, until they were all politely applauding their boss. Suddenly the big man grinned, revealing blackened stumps for teeth. Then, just as suddenly bored, he flapped his hand, signalling them to leave. Ben grabbed Valentina and rushed her back to the train door. Carrie was leaning out of the window waving.

'Alexei said you'd been arrested,' she panted. 'What happened?'

Valentina could see Alexei and two of his friends from the previous evening leaning out of the window in a compartment further up the train. She waved shyly at him, rewarded by one of his wonderful smiles.

'Nothing we couldn't handle. Right, Vally?' Then, noticing her attention was elsewhere, he asked, 'Who are those guys?'

Carrie led them down the corridor, talking excitedly. 'We met them last night. The drop-dead gorgeous one, Alexei, was dancing with Valentina in the saloon bar. Can you believe,' she turned around with a shocked face, 'that Vally actually fell asleep sitting beside him! Anyway, lucky for us, he overheard the soldiers talking, realised we were in trouble and organised a bribe. Something to do with having no visa.' She flung open their compartment door, steadying herself against the sudden movement as the train started up again. 'So with Alexei's bribe, they let you go!' She grinned delightedly.

'And I thought it was because of my quick wit and trendy sunnies. Well, I'll have to ask for them back. I'll need them for snowboarding.' He made as if to leave again, before adding, 'Only joking!'

'You'd better be,' Valentina grimaced. 'My palms are sweating and my heart rate's in over-drive. Do you realise how close we were to serious trouble?'

Ben grinned. 'It was good. My first border dispute. Will we get to see a real revolution? Maybe a peasant revolt?'

'You're revolting.' Carrie picked up his sweaty socks, lying on the floor. 'Not like Alexei. Isn't he the hottest babe you've ever seen?'

Valentina nodded dumbly. She was still

reeling from her brush with the authorities. It was amazing to her how innocent Carrie and Ben were. They seemed to have no comprehension of how close they had come to being arrested. Growing up in Australia, they could never begin to understand the power of corrupt authorities. But Alexei knew. He'd saved her life. Her heart flared with warmth for him. 'Listen, both of you, under no circumstances tell Mama about that incident. She will go off her tree.'

There was a short rap on the door. Valentina tensed instinctively. Ben opened the door.

'Oh,' he said, unenthusiastically.

Alexei stood at the door holding Valentina's shoes, smiling over Ben's shoulder at her. She sat down quickly, her knees turning to jelly again.

'It's Prince Charming,' said Ben, 'with a pair of glass slippers.'

'Hi, come in,' cried Carrie, and pushed forward to give him one of her long New Age hugs. Alexei caught Valentina's eye. She thought she discerned the slightest of winks.

'You leave your shoes in our compartment last night.' He handed them over. 'We enjoy ourselves, no?'

Valentina blushed.

Ben watched her curiously, then put out his hand. 'Thanks, mate. My sister tells me you bribed the guy.'

Alexei ignored it and took him in a bear hug instead. 'My Afstrylyan brother,' he replied. 'Don't mention it. I only want to help. Anyway, is your money.'

'What?'

Carrie looked embarrassed. 'We needed a bribe and you had American dollars. So I took ...'

Ben flipped open his empty wallet, and choked. 'All of it, *and* my Raybans?'

Alexei shrugged. 'They could have detained you for weeks. I had no option. Your beautiful sister helped me find the money.' He beamed at her. 'And I spoke to Pavel, one of the soldiers. You were lucky; Pavel is from my country. He took the bribe to the commandant. Otherwise ...?' he lifted his hands eloquently.

Valentina could not take her eyes off his face. 'Thank you so much, Alexei. I don't know what we would have done without you.' Her cheeks flamed with pleasure.

'We're all grateful,' Carrie joined in. She tossed her hair coquettishly over her shoulder and licked her lips.

Alexei stared first at Valentina, then Carrie. His face expressed infinite regret.

Alexei bowed low over Valentina's hand and kissed her. She felt his lips drain the strength out of her body. Then gallantly, he did the same to Carrie. Seconds later he was gone. A huge lump swelled up in her throat and down into her stomach. Would she ever see him again?

Ben slammed the door shut. 'Well, that's the sleazeball gone.'

'How dare you?' Carrie turned on him. 'If it wasn't for Alexei, you'd both be on your way to Siberia. Of all the ungrateful . . . '

'I'm not ungrateful,' Ben protested. 'It was just the vomit-making way you two rolled over and panted like a pair of well-trained poodles.'

'I'm a Post-Modern Feminist and I resent being called a dog,' Carrie fumed. 'And Vally's never fallen for a guy in her life, you know that. She's immune to anyone who isn't in tights and twice her age.'

Valentina felt an upsurge of resentment. It was true, she only ever seemed to have crushes on older men; but the fact they had all been teachers or choreographers was because those were the only men she met.

'Alexei got us out of trouble and we'll never see him again, so let's not fight over it.' She kept her voice calm.

'It's okay for you to be so cool,' Carrie howled, 'Miss Snow Princess! And as for you, you insensitive brain-dead surfing bogan . . . ' She threw one of Valentina's shoes at Ben, then flung herself on the bunk. 'I've just said goodbye to the man of my dreams!' And she let out a long wail of agony.

# 5

They stumbled out on to the platform. Valentina noticed everyone had changed into heavy overcoats and fur hats. She felt seasick walking on solid ground after so long on the train. And the deafening rush of people, the maze of exits and corridors confused her even more.

'We have to find the Metro,' said Valentina, struggling to decipher the Cyrillic lettering on a large sign. She gazed anxiously around her as they trudged in the general direction of an underground pass. There were tunnels, escalators, staircases and lifts in all directions. 'This looks like the escalator out,' said Ben. They stepped onto an antique moving staircase, with filigree wrought-iron banisters and oak-slatted steps. It reached up out of the bowels of the station, hundreds of feet towards daylight.

'It's the stairway to Heaven.' A sad smile lit

up Carrie's face as they floated up into the daylight.

At the top they found a vast plate-glass window through which they could see the streets of Moscow. Just outside the doors stood a frighteningly large statue of Lenin. Swinging glass doors swished apart and closed again as people came and went. Clouds of frozen air hit them in waves.

'If we go out there now,' Ben muttered, 'we'll crumble into frozen chips of ice.'

They stared aghast at the wind-flattened people, layered in fur, faces mute with cold.

'I'm not going out there until we know exactly what we're doing. I reckon we'd have about ten minutes before we'd seize up and keel over.' At last Carrie had her mind on something else besides Alexei.

Valentina peered at the building across the street. 'I can see a sign. I think it says the Hotel Metropol.'

'How far?' Carrie was short-sighted.

'Two minutes at a run.'

'I'll carry the two heavy bags.' Ben shouldered the biggest one and heaved the other up off the trolley. 'Let's go!'

They swept out, flinching as the bitter wind filled their lungs. Dodging the traffic, they dashed across the road, scrambled up the steps and fell through the revolving doors of the Hotel Metropol into another world – into another century.

'Pinch me! Is this real?' Ben dropped his bags and his jaw.

The setting was perfect. Rich silk Persian carpets underfoot, gilded arches above, painted alcoves around. An orchestra played Vivaldi amongst huge tropical palms. Waiters shimmied past with tea and vodka. Wealthy middle-aged couples waltzed in feather boas and black tail suits.

So that's where my mother gets her dress sense, thought Valentina, worried by the glamour. This place will cost a fortune! She made her way bravely to the reception and asked for a rates card. It was worse than she thought.

'It's going to cost more for one night than we'd budgeted for the whole five days! So don't get comfortable,' she warned Ben, who'd started nibbling the free nuts.

'It's only money; it's just a form of energy. And there's always more,' assured Carrie. She was taking off her coat and enjoying the attention her stunning svelte figure had on a group of business-men nearby. She looked elegant, her face brave in suffering as she posed at the reception desk. She made the Russian women around her look hope-lessly overweight. 'If I'm going to suffer, I might as well be comfortable at the same time.'

'But we won't have enough money for the whole troupe to stay here!'

'Why don't we stay here until the others come? That'll give us time to acclimatise, find somewhere else cheaper, and have a great time while Dragon Woman is not here.'

Valentina didn't rise to the bait. Her mother

seemed so far away now, it was a waste of time defending her. And there was some merit in Ben's argument. They certainly couldn't find anywhere else tonight. Relenting, she signed them in, saving money by booking a twin for her and Carrie. Noticing a fax machine, she also wrote two faxes – one to her mother and one to the Artistic Director of the Bolshoi, telling them they'd arrived.

The girls' room was on the third floor, giving them an excuse to use the original, pre-Lenin lift. They left Ben rising up to his own room, looking like a prisoner in a floating wrought-iron jail.

Their room was a revelation. 'I can't believe the furniture here. It's like staying in a museum. Did you live like this in Moscow?' Carrie threw down her bags and rushed to examine the antiques. From the carved four-poster beds to the inlaid oak panelling, the room was a stage set for *La Dame aux Camélias*.

'No. No one does,' Valentina remembered dull granite blocks of flats with small rooms and the cold, echoing stairways smelling of cabbage.

'Look at this bathroom! Gold taps and cherubs on the ceiling! I'm going to plunge myself in scalding water and purge myself of the pain of unrequited love.'

Valentina heard the pounding of hot water on porcelain. Steam billowed from the door. The phone rang – a large ornate, gold phone.

'Hi, it's me. I'm too starving to wait for you guys; I'll see you in the restaurant.' Ben hung up.

Valentina listened to Carrie singing 'I will always love you' in the bathroom, with a Whitney Houston long throb in her voice.

She didn't feel hungry. She didn't feel anything. Moscow frost had already settled on her heart. Slowly, she unpacked her bags and Carrie's, carefully hanging their things in the wardrobes and tidying away their shoes and wallets. The shoes Alexei had returned to her needed polishing. Finding the bag of cleaning things, she set about rubbing black cream into the heels, thrusting her fingers into the toes for support.

Something hard in the toe! She pulled out a twist of paper and smoothed it flat.

*Dear Valentina*, she read. *I hope you read this while you are still in Moscow. I want to tell you how beautiful you are, I am pregnant with joy to have met you. If you have time, call me on 08356278 and I will come to you. Maybe I can help you find the church where your babushka buried her husband?*

*We will meet again. Is fate.*

*Your Alexei.*

Trembling with joy, she folded it into a tiny cube and hid it inside her bra.

'Your turn,' sang out Carrie, wrapped in a fluffy cream towelling robe and rubbing the long hair dripping down her back.

Valentina fled into the bathroom, stripped off her clothes and plunged herself into the deep, foaming bath. Her thoughts were in a frenzy. He wanted her. She couldn't somehow believe it. All her life she'd locked up the part of her heart that wanted love. When she'd felt the heat of attraction, she deliberately put it out with work and more work and more work. It was Mama's answer to everything. And it protected her from the sort of muddles Carrie got involved in.

Valentina had too much self-discipline for that. Or did she? Would she be able to hold back if Alexei wanted her? She felt his hand on her breast and shivered. No, this time there could be no holding back. She knew it. So she must totally avoid him. Right?

'Valentina!' She heard Carrie's muffled cry from the bedroom.

Wearily, she towelled off, wrapped her hair in an enormous turban and emerged to find Carrie sprawled across the bed, weeping. She was half-dressed, her tangle of corn-coloured hair fanning out on the turquoise bedspread. 'I . . . am . . . so . . . unhappy,' she hiccupped through a blocked nose. Twisting round to face Valentina, her face a swollen red mass of tears, she held out her arms for a hug.

They sat for a moment, rocking, Valentina stroking back her damp hair, Carrie gasping for breath. 'It's all right; you'll get over it. There are plenty more gorgeous men. There may be one downstairs now, in the dining room, waiting to meet you.'

Carrie giggled weakly, and the phone rang

again. Disentangling herself, Valentina picked up the receiver.

'Me again. When are you pair showing? I've already eaten a smoked salmon and three bowls of onion soup. I'm bored. Come and cheer me up.'

'We'll be down in a minute.' She replaced the receiver. Carrie had gone into the bathroom to splash her face. Valentina found herself mechanically tidying the room. She fussed with her clothes, dressing carefully, smoothing out the bedspread. One part of her desperately wanted to call Alexei, just to hear his voice again – maybe even to ask him to help her find the Cathedral of Our Lady of Smolensk. He could guide her through the maze of difficulties she'd be sure to encounter in this city. But her mother would be here in a day or two, and that would squash any chance they had of being together. And in any case, how could she possibly meet him behind Carrie's back?

*Oh, Alexei! Alexei! Alexei!* She bit her knuckles to distract herself from the pain in her heart. Blood welled from the teeth marks.

Carrie emerged wearing fresh lip gloss. 'You've scratched yourself! I've got some plasters, here in my . . . Oh you gorgeous thing, you've tidied away all my stuff.' She carefully stuck the plaster on Valentina's knuckle and, seeing the exhausted look on her face, added 'Oh, Val, here am I whinge-ing on about some man. You've got the whole weight of this performance on your mind, all the organisation to do, your mother about to arrive . . .

that would be enough to freak anyone out. You are so fantastic, so strong. I wish I were more like you.' Her eyes shone with frank admiration.

'We'd better hurry up; Ben has been on the phone twice. He's eating our entire kitty down there – we have to protect our financial position.'

'I hope he makes himself sick. Who'd have thought he could be so petty and jealous. All those nasty comments about Alexei! I'll kill him if he starts again.' She pulled on her boots with a ferocious kick.

'I'm sure he didn't mean to upset you.'

'No, he never means anything. That's the trouble with Ben. All my life he's been the successful one. Teachers always sat us together because we were twins. They thought we'd want to be with each other. But do you have any idea what it's like to have someone like Ben around all day? He beat me at every subject, and he never did any work. Never read a book in his life. Apparently he walked before me, talked before me. He was even born two minutes earlier. Then, when he joined my ballet class, he was better than me almost straight-away.'

Valentina smiled. 'I know. I can never believe how quickly he picks up steps, and I have to work so hard all the time. He can goof off and surf all night and still be fresh and strong. Life just isn't fair, is it?' She locked their door and followed Carrie out to the lift.

# 6

'Did you sleep well?' Ben asked, on his best behaviour. They were eating breakfast in the Hall of Golden Mirrors dining room. He was still dressed for the beach in track pants and T-shirt.

'Perfectly, thank you,' his sister replied, exuding patchouli oil and draped in the elegant cape she bought in Budapest.

'Any dreams?' he asked innocently.

'If you mean . . . ' she fumed.

But Valentina stopped them. 'Enough of all that. Alexei is history.' She spoke more emphatically than she meant to, trying to convince herself. 'We've got a lot on today. First, Ben, we've got to get over to the Bolshoi. Carrie, you'll have to spend the morning finding another hotel. The street directories and tourist lists are in our room, and the receptionist will help you. Ben, I've had a reply

76

from the Artistic Director, Stephan Orlovsky. We meet him at nine this morning.'

They finished their sweet rolls and coffee in silence and rugged up to brave the morning air. Snow had broken the frost that morning, sending lazy fat flakes spinning out of the sky. Ben pulled up the hood on his jacket and Valentina was glad she'd bought the gloves and hat. Holding up her face to the snow, she opened her mouth to catch a snowflake.

'I wish I had a camera.' Ben gazed at her affectionately.

'You can buy postcards,' Valentina answered, straightening her head to look at the view of Pushkin Square.

Ben took her hand and led her across the road, dodging cars and great grey piles of slush. The heat of the Metro was welcome, sucking them down into its warm underbelly. This time Valentina had a good idea where to go, having studied maps the night before. Within twenty minutes they were back up on the street, standing in front of the Bolshoi. A thin ray of lemony sunshine glittered on the gold cupolas, giving them a dream-like quality.

They held their breath in awe.

'I've dreamed about this, seen photographs – but it's better than I ever could have imagined.'

Ben nodded, understanding. 'It's filth.'

'In three days, we'll be dancing on the stage, as principals,' she breathed.

'Better than a four-metre swell at Suicide Bay.

Val,' he laughed suddenly, picking her up and tossing her several feet into the air, 'we're legends!'

A bearded man bundled in coats, tied in the middle with several scarves, approached Ben. 'Congratulations.' He held out his hand.

'Thank you, mate.' Ben shook it warmly, looking puzzled.

'Nice jeans,' the man added, squinting down at his legs.

'What?'

'My son always asking me for a pair. Would you sell them perhaps?'

'Later.' Ben turned to follow Valentina up the marble steps of the world's greatest theatre.

'Then what about changing some dollars for roubles?' the old man shouted, as they disappeared into the grand entrance.

Inside the theatre foyer, the level of opulence put the Hotel Metropol to shame. 'Everything here was built before the revolution. So beautiful,' whispered Valentina as they padded across the velvety red carpet. A small bespectacled man sat behind a wall of polished mahogany at the reception desk. He asked who they wanted in Russian, and Valentina was able to reply. Her Russian was improving. She asked for Stephan Orlovsky, the Artistic Director.

'I love it when you talk like that,' Ben grinned. 'It's a sing-song sound. Suits you.'

For the first time, Valentina was aware she wasn't Australian. She felt somehow at ease in this language. The horrible cold, the strange dangerous soldiers, even the dull grey housing blocks seemed oddly familiar – like coming home.

'Valentina Laputin!' A man in a tail coat rushed towards them. 'I was expecting you, but I would have recognised you anyway.'

'But I don't look like my mother.' She was shocked. No one had ever said that before.

'Ah.' He suddenly seemed embarrassed, then held out his arms to embrace her. 'It is only a look in the eyes. Anya and I danced together, many years ago. Before you were born. She was extraordinary, so dedicated and controlled. She calls herself Anya Laputin now?'

Valentina nodded, surprised. 'Of course. She married; did you know her as Anya Pavrych?'

Orlovsky paused. He was wearing gold-rimmed spectacles and sparkles of light flickered, obscuring his eyes. Then he looked away, abruptly shuffling the papers he carried. 'Come then, I was expecting you. And Mr Benjamin Frazer. Welcome to Moscow. Follow me.' He bustled up a flight of white marble stairs, past gilt-framed oil paintings of dancers. She recognised some of them, Pavlova in *Swan Lake*, Nureyev in *Nutcracker*. Longing to have a closer look, she had to run to keep up with Orlovsky and answer the flood of questions.

By the time they reached his office, she'd answered a series of questions about their production of *Romeo*, about Madame's Dance Academy in Sydney, what the weather was like in Australia and the average price of houses. Valentina needed information from him, and as she worked through her list she noticed Ben getting restless.

'Do you mind if I go down to the studio?' he finally asked. 'I want to stretch out and warm up my muscles.'

'Okay. I'll see you later.' Valentina hadn't finished briefing Orlovsky. And there was something else.

'When did you know my mother?' she asked as soon as Ben left.

'In 1975, when she first came to Moscow.'

'So you did know she was married?'

'Yes. She married someone wealthy, but she never mentioned him. He never turned up at our parties. I expect he was too busy with important affairs.' Then, noticing her stricken expression, he added, 'I'm so sorry.'

'Is he still here, in Moscow?'

Tiny rainbows of light glittered around his face. 'I believe he is, but I can tell you no more. One thing we have learnt from the Communists is discretion. You must ask Anya,' he added firmly. 'Now my assistant will show you round the theatre. Good luck; I look forward to the show.'

'Thank you.' Valentina stood up. 'Just his name ... please?'

'The past is gone. Learn to forget it. We have.'

She turned to leave.

'And Valentina ...'

She paused hopefully at the doorway. 'Yes?'

'So sorry we caused you these problems with the booking ... ' He lifted his shoulders delicately in remorse.

'How is everything?' Ben was in a heated, mirror-walled studio, working at the *barre*, stripped down to his shorts. His lithe, golden-skinned body reflected back endlessly, a million Bens mirroring back into the cosmos. She wondered how she would react if she came upon Alexei in this studio.

'Bad,' she answered, 'for me, that is. Everything else is fine.

He stopped immediately. 'You asked about your father?'

'He's here now, in Moscow. But Orlovsky won't give me a name. He says the past is gone, to forget it.'

Ben pulled on his clothes. 'He could be right. There might be a good reason for all this secrecy.'

'If he's dead, I want to know, then I can forget about him. If he's alive, I have a right to meet him. Do you think I'm being unreasonable?'

'No. I think you need to find him, so that you can get on with the rest of your life. As long as he's missing, there's a hole in your heart so big no man will ever be able to fill it.'

Valentina thought of Alexei. Would he have replaced this old, old longing? A wave of sadness washed over her. She'd never know.

'Hey, don't worry. We'll start this afternoon

looking for the church Babushka told you about. I'm sure there was some clue there; she was trying to help you.'

'I can't. I have to talk to the publicity people, and costumes and props. I'll be lucky if I get back by five.'

'Could I start looking up Gallianos in the telephone directory?'

'You can't read Cyrillic. We'll go tonight, after dinner. Come on, let's see how Carrie got on,' and they headed off back to the Metropol.


After lunch, Valentina decided to walk to the theatre. She needed a workout and it had stopped snowing. She left Ben and Carrie dancing to 'Rock around the Clock', played by a five-piece combo in the hotel lounge, surrounded by large clumsy couples bouncing off each other like pinballs.

The snow was melting as she skidded along the pavements that led to the Kremlin, past the famous GUM fashion department store. She paused, fascinated by the models in the store window. They looked as though they'd been dressed by the Salvation Army and their hair carved by a stonemason. Hurrying into Red Square, she was aghast at the heroic ugliness of the Kremlin walls, the colour of stale frozen meat – vast, frost-flecked prison walls. Another oversized statue of Lenin glowered down at her, reminding her of the problems she had to sort out, making her feel guilty for pigging out in

Budapest, for buying sexy satin lingerie, for kissing Alexei, for thinking about him incessantly, for being a bad daughter and defying her mother. Basically, for living.

She turned thankfully out of the square and up towards Kuznetsky Bridge. And there, facing her, stood the Bolshoi, so beautiful it took her breath away all over again. A woman looking like a sack of cabbages was selling spring violets. Valentina thought of Babushka, and bought a bunch.

'Now you have good luck,' croaked the woman.

Valentina replied that she needed all the luck she could get, and hurried on into the theatre.

The props man Orlovsky had organised for her to meet was late. In fact, he wasn't there, and no one had any idea where he could be. It was dark in the underground props area, so Valentina flopped down to wait amongst the piles of painted flats, watching a cleaning lady sweep slowly around four-poster beds, Roman columns, mock turrets, bucolic wheelbarrows of dried flowers, velvet armchairs and sedans – the dusty symbols of a thousand performances.

The cleaner was seized by a paroxysm of coughing, which she cured by lighting up a full-strength cigarette. Valentina asked if she were all right.

'Would be if I didn't have to do everything around here,' she complained.

'You're in props?' asked Valentina, jumping up.

'Assistant, but I should be the boss. He's always at the vodka. Russian men.' She shook her head in disgust.

'Fantastic!' She put out her hand. 'My name's Valentina Galliano, and we're on at the end of the week, in *Romeo and Juliet*. Are the sets ready?'

The old woman guffawed, choked, coughed and re-lit her cigarette, all at the same time. 'Next week, you say?'

It wasn't easy, but with Valentina's copy of the technical script and Olga's help, they managed to find most of what they needed. Several hours later, with many of the props and most of the flats identified and labelled, Valentina emerged from the basement to look for Orlovsky. She needed his written permission before the lighting people would accept directions. And the costume lady pretended she didn't understand her Russian. She was too busy guzzling baclavas and pouring cups of tea for the New York Ballet people. All over the offices and studios of the Bolshoi, Valentina came across Americans talking loudly, dressed in the understated elegance of the seriously rich. They looked pityingly at Valentina as if she were a poor local *corps-de-ballet* member who had strayed.

Some of them were on the main stage, rehearsing *Coppelia*. Valentina crept into the stalls to watch. It was her first time in the auditorium, and she was frozen with awe. The domed ceiling rose like the heavens, painted with Byzantine images of legendary figures. Heavy chandeliers like clouds of diamonds floated above her. And all around, golden cherubs played their harps and flutes. *How wonderful*, she thought comparing them with the angry stone Lenins scowling all over Red Square. The Russians must have had their revolution because they were blissed out with too much culture. The poor things didn't realise how bad the opposite extreme would be.

A small rehearsal orchestra was tuning up as the principals stretched and turned, waiting for their cue. It was too late to watch for long, but Valentina was madly impressed by the little she did see. The girl was wonderful, tightly controlled, but as light as a butterfly. She didn't think the boy was as powerful as Ben, but then few dancers had the sort of casual charisma Ben gave out without realising. It was as if he didn't really care what anyone thought of him; he was just dancing for the sheer joy of exercising his magnificent body, whereas Alexei danced consciously. He deliberately used his eyes, his face, his hands, his body to seduce his audience, to master their response. She shuddered. It was time to go.

She found Carrie in their room, scribbling at the desk.

'Did you find anything?' she called out, pulling off her boots and coat.

'Yep. You'll hate it, but it's a quarter of the

price of this place, near the theatre and clean enough. It's called the Hotel of the Fallen Heroes. Have you noticed there are only stunning, pre-revolutionary buildings here or dismal concrete blocks. Do you suppose Russia is schizophrenic?'

Valentina thought of Mama. 'It's possible. Anyway, well done. We'll move in when the others arrive. Where's Ben?'

'I don't know. He was deep in discussion with a team of snowboarders from Iceland when I set off this afternoon.'

'Well I hope he isn't trying to be a hero somewhere. You don't suppose he would have gone out with them, do you . . . '

Carrie's face fell. 'No question he would. There was that look in his eye. But don't worry, Ben's like a cat; he always lands on his feet. He's never had an accident yet.'

Valentina felt uneasy. 'Shall we wait for him for dinner?'

'I'm not eating; it's a fast day. How did you get on?'

'Sets and sound are fixed up. I've got a few problems still with costumes and publicity – otherwise okay. But I did get a chance to ask Orlovsky about my father. He danced with Mama and knew a lot more than he was willing to say. He told me to forget the past. But I know Papa's alive now, and living in Moscow, I suspect. It all gets weirder and weirder.'

'Did he know any of her family or friends?'

'He didn't say.'

'Maybe she liked to keep work and her private life separate.'

'Mm. I wonder if it would be any good calling Babushka.'

'If she's kept your mother's secret all these years, why would she talk to you now? And maybe your mother has a good reason for keeping you apart. Like your Dad is married to someone else and your appearance could upset her. Or he's in prison?'

'Orlovsky said he was wealthy.'

'Val.' Carrie sat on the bed beside her, pulling her close. 'Sometimes it's better to accept life the way it is – to trust everything's working out the way it should.'

'You mean just forget about him?'

Carrie sighed. 'I know it's hard. I've been trying to forget Alexei.' She pulled out her blue book for inspiration. 'There's a line here I've been chanting to myself. *Go into the sadness, appreciate its beauty*,' she read. 'But the only beauty I can appreciate just now is Alexei's, so it hasn't really helped.' She blew her nose. 'I know, why don't we go down to the cemetery and take those violets, like Babushka asked you to. Ben'll be here when we get back.'

Valentina agreed, struggling wearily to her feet and reaching for her coat. Collecting the street maps, they set off in the cold, early evening air. Streetlights were being turned on, casting a dull, phosphorescent-orange glow on the piles of melting snow. They hailed the first taxi they saw, and set off to the water meadows on the outskirts of Moscow.

The road took them out through the medieval parts of Moscow, the ancient fortifications of Kitai-Garod that circled the city like a necklace. In the dying light, they could see water flickering from the bend of the Moskva River, where the ghostly white cupolas of Our Lady of Smolensk rose out of the flat plain.

Several minutes later, they turned into a beautiful old square, dominated by the cathedral. Valentina paid off the driver and they stood, staggered by the sheer size of the building.

'Lets go in and meditate. The energy here feels fantastic.'

'No, we have to find another church, a much smaller one. Come on.'

They set off down a narrow, cobblestone side street. A beetroot seller broiling small beets over a charcoal fire called out to them. The smell reminded Valentina of Babushka's cooking and they stopped to buy a dish. She watched him pouring yoghurt over the crimson beets and asked about the small church.

'Ah. Is gone. In its place they build the Hall of the Committee for Re-Education.'

Valentina was frantic. 'But where was the Church, before they pulled it down?'

'Over there,' he pointed a blunt fingernail. 'By

that wasteground. There was a cemetery beside it, I think.'

They hurried over the square, slipping and slithering on the pavestones and clutching each other for support, until they reached a sad patch of weeds, half hidden by mounds of melting snow. Moss and lichen covered the few gravestones heaped on top of each other on one side. A few broken headstones lay among the weeds.

'Thank heavens Babushka isn't here. She'd be so disappointed.' Valentina put down her things and began to poke around the rubble. 'There should be a gravestone here, with my grandfather's name, Ivan Igorovich Pavrych. It should look like this,' and she scribbled the Cyrillic letters on a piece of paper for Carrie.

'This will be impossible, but if you're determined,' Carrie sighed, and she got to work. And it was Carrie who found it, over an hour later. Sitting down to recover her breath after an hour of heaving stones and peering about while they flared matches for light, she thought the ground felt too even. 'There's another one here,' she cried out, jumping off the stone, and rubbing at the moss with her gloved hands.

'Is this the one?' called Carrie.

*Here lies Ivan Igorovich Galliano*, read Valentina, *beloved husband of Irena Stefanovna, father of Anya Ivanovna and Viktor Ivanovich.*

'Yes! Look! Ivan Igorovich ... Galliano. They told me Galliano was my father's name. But it's hers. It's Mama's family name! Babushka always said her husband's name was Ivan Pavrych. Why would she say that?'

'Maybe that was her own family name, before she married your grandfather.'

'Yes. And she's been helping my mother cover up something. How horrible; they've all been lying.

'And Viktor? I didn't know I had an uncle!' She spun round to face Carrie. 'Why on earth would she have hidden her brother from me? And Babushka? She always said she only had one child.'

'She must have had a reason.' Carrie was exhausted. 'My toes disappeared hours ago. Can't we go home now?'

Valentina knelt on the muddy ground, rubbing at the stone with her bare hands. 'No. I have to get the moss off. I promised Babushka.' A huge lump formed in her throat as she rubbed her frozen fingers across the names of her family. So many secrets, so many lies. Viktor. Viktor. Who is he, where is he? What could he tell her?

Then, tenderly, she laid the crumpled violets on the grave of Ivan Galliano, the shoemaker who once ate kasha on the Yvshenko Bridge, and picked violets in the spring with a young dancer called Irena Pavrych.

'So Galliano was your mother's name, not your father's. Maybe she wasn't even married?' Carrie was concerned for her friend.

'She was. Orlovsky admitted as much.' They were in a taxi, bumping back to the Hotel Metropol.

'We're worse off than we were before.'

Valentina rolled down her window an inch; she was suffocating. 'No, we're better off. We have Viktor's name, and we know my father is alive and in Moscow.'

'How will you find Viktor Galliano? He could be anywhere.' Carrie privately marvelled at Valentina's persistence.

'His father – my grandfather, Ivan – made ballet shoes for the Bolshoi. It was a successful business; I know Babushka was sorry to leave it when they came to Australia. Maybe it's still going and someone knows something. After all, lots of people in those days learnt their trade from their fathers. He might still be in the business.'

'Bit of a long shot, isn't it?' Valentina was lost in thought. She needed help if she was going to find her uncle before Mama arrived. There was so little time. She and Ben were scheduled to rehearse Act Two of *Romeo* tomorrow. Pushing her hand into her pocket, she curled her numb fingers around the piece of paper with Alexei's number on it. He would come if she called; he would help her. She was sure of that. Outside the stars shone like candle flames on black velvet.

'Look,' Carrie pointed, 'Orion's girdle is upside down.'

'That's because we're in the Northern Hemisphere.'

'I feel upside down too,' Carrie sighed. 'Do you think I'll ever see him again?'

Valentina felt a pang of disloyalty.

'I honestly feel I would die if I never saw him again.'

Valentina thought of all the times she'd heard Carrie say the same words – how many guys she'd fallen for and then dropped. But guilt gripped her heart all the same. She quietly slipped the piece of paper out of the window. Gone. It disappeared as if it had never existed. No more temptation. She ought to have felt proud of herself, but all she could see were his eyes, piercing hers, saying 'It's fate'.

'Do you think we'll see him again?' Carrie persisted.

'Only if it's meant to be,' she sighed, imitating Carrie's voice as she spoke. 'Why don't you send out one of your pink balloons?'

'Hey, great idea.' Carrie cheered up.

As they waved away the taxi driver and climbed the steps up to the Hotel Metropol, they could hear the lounge combo playing 'I still call Australia home'.

'Ben's back,' said Valentina, as they ducked under the potted plants. They found him nursing a beer in the lounge, looking sombre.

He looked up. 'Do you want the good news or the bad?'

'You've taught the band a new song,' Carrie smiled. Then, as he shook his head, she shouted joyfully, 'You've found Alexei?'

'That would be bad news. No, I got some snowboarding in before the snows melted. Apparently the temperature is going up from tonight. Spring is here at last.'

'And the bad?' Valentina's heart thudded.

Slowly Ben withdrew his arm, which had been covered by the jacket draped over his shoulder. It was in a sling.

'I hurt my wrist.' His innocent topaz eyes gazed up at them, filled with remorse.

# 7

'I can't believe it. You fool! Going out to play in the snow, like a child. Wrecking everything we've all worked towards. Stupid baby!' Carrie flung herself into an armchair.

'Am not.'

'Are so!'

'Please!' Valentina clutched her forehead. A vein was throbbing like a heartbeat. 'How bad is it, Ben?'

'I saw a doctor this afternoon, after we got back. He thinks it's a sprain, but it could be a green-stick fracture. By the way,' his face lit up for a moment, 'have you any idea how incredible snow-boarding is? Like surfing a mountain ...'

'Have you any idea how much trouble we could be in?' Valentina interrupted.

His face fell. 'Dr Vlad said I couldn't lift any

heavy weights. He bound it up.' He held up his bandaged arm.

Valentina's head began to swim. 'So you can't lift me.'

Their eyes met. In the background a singer with a heavy Russian accent sang: *When all of your sheeps come back to your shows, and I realise something I've always known, I steel call Austrylya, I still call . . .*

'We won't be going back to Australia ever, if this is true. Tell me it's a practical joke, Ben. You're just winding me up, aren't you?'

He shook his head, dumbly.

'Perhaps I could try rubbing in some tea-tree oil.' Carrie reached out towards him.

'Don't come near me with your snake oil! It really hurts. God, I'm so sorry, guys. You've no idea how sorry I am.' He hunched in his chair, too miserable to speak. Valentina almost felt sorry for him.

'Vlad'll be here in a minute. He's coming to give me an injection to bring down the swelling.'

'Oh God,' moaned Carrie.

*Mama, I so wish you were here now*, thought Valentina.

*I steel call Austrylya home*, yelled the singer in a final blast of misplaced patriotic fervour.


Dr Vlad came shortly after and injected Ben with a hypodermic so large, Ben called him Vlad the

Impaler. He also delivered his final verdict. Under no circumstances was Ben to dance tomorrow, or for the rest of the week, if it involved lifting Valentina. When Vlad left, nobody could bear to speak. They went silently to their rooms, sleeping fitfully and dreading the morning.

A fax arrived at the reception desk as they were all leaving for the Bolshoi after breakfast.

*How are you, my darlings? So glad you have arranged everything so beautifully and I look forward to seeing how much you have improved your pas-de-deux.*

*Ben, stay away from the snow, and Valentina, do not even speak to any of the dancers, I know what deceiving flirts they can be. I arrive at 8.00 a.m., Moscow time, tomorrow morning. We all arrive together. Love and kisses, Mama.*

'Oh, God, I think I'm going to be sick.' Valentina's face paled.

'It's not your fault I've been a bloody idiot.' Ben looked miserable. 'I'll tell her you've done a brilliant job in getting everything organised.'

'You think she'll even listen to you, or to any of us?' Valentina almost wept.

'Cool it, Val. It was an accident. These things happen.' Carrie took her hand and led her out into the street. 'We've got to find an understudy, now, just in case Ben really can't dance on Friday.'

'Which of course I will. Try stopping me,' he smiled, taking her other hand. 'Doctors aren't prophets. He wouldn't know what a legend I am. I never feel pain. Ask Carrie.'

'Ben doesn't feel anything, unfortunately, particularly a sense of responsibility, or he'd never have gone out with those guys. They were Olympic snowboarders!'

'It's a slight sprain, no big deal. Get off my case, Carrie.'

Valentina looked up wearily at the sky. A pale watery sun struggled to break the clouds, painting the snow cream and brightening the faces scurrying past.

'Look,' Ben pulled down his beanie, 'those guys were right. The snow's melting. We'll be sun-baking soon!'

They found their way back to the theatre, and up to Orlovsky's office. He was sympathetic and unperturbed.

'Let me see.' He scrabbled amongst a pile of documents on his desk. 'I'll check if any of our young *corps-de-ballet* boys are free. No, they all seem to be involved with the Americans. But leave it with me; there are plenty of final-year Academy boys around. I may be able to find one who's danced Romeo before. Off you go to your studio, and don't worry.'

Valentina stripped in the changing rooms. She scraped her hair back, wincing in pain as she bound it tightly into a knot. Trying to pin back the last escaping tendrils, she heard Carrie clatter in behind her.

'Guess what!' Her face had turned puce and her eyes shone like halogen lamps. 'I've just seen him – Alexei! He was going into the men's rooms. I'm going back there now, to lay an ambush. See ya.' And she was gone.

Valentina dropped the packet of hair grips. Bending to pick them up, she found her hands trembling and her fingers as numb and useless as a bunch of sausages. *Must be the cold*, she muttered through chattering teeth. Her stomach heaved as she straightened up and took a last look at herself. The men's rooms lay to her left. If she darted down the right corridor, she could escape any chance of bumping into him. There were dozens of rehearsal studios here; she'd be safe enough.

The corridors were empty, apart from a group of American girls giggling. She thought she heard Alexei's name spoken, but decided she was becoming paranoid. Up a flight of stairs, she found the same mirrored studio, with Ben, stretching out, dressed for work.

Relieved, she gasped, 'What are you doing?'

'I'll work beside you. I won't lift, just walk you through.'

She was grateful; his presence comforted her. She longed to ask for a cuddle, just for reassurance, but she knew how he felt about Alexei.

'Where's Carrie?'

'Not sure,' she lied, switching on a tape of the

second act *pas-de-deux*. For ten minutes she warmed up slowly, easing herself into the steps, leaning on Ben's good arm, stretching up on *pointe*.

'My toe's much better,' she murmured as she held the pose.

'Pity your control isn't. What's the matter, Val?'

He was right. The shaking she'd felt in the changing rooms had intensified.

Suddenly the studio door opened and there stood Alexei, dressed in white tights, a short brocade waistcoat and the fine cotton, full-sleeved shirt of the classical Romeo. His hair, smooth as buttered silk, was brushed off his face and flowed over his collar. Expressionless, his beautiful profile with its high Tartar cheekbones and full sensual mouth reflected endlessly in the mirrors. *It's fate.*

Carrie crept in behind him, her face wreathed in smiles.

'So you're the stand-in.' Ben scowled. 'Well, it's not a dress rehearsal. And we're doing *Romeo*, not *Don Juan*.' He stood back reluctantly as Alexei bowed to Valentina.

'Where do you guys want to go from?' Carrie trotted over to the tape machine, hissing at Ben as she passed, 'Run along and play in the snow.'

'From the beginning.' Alexei looked deep into Valentina's eyes. 'I need a full run-through. Perhaps you,' he twinkled at Carrie, 'could give me the cues in the crowd scenes. And you,' he bowed gallantly at Ben, 'please, stay over there. I should be grateful for your comments later.'

Valentina watched entranced as he moved through the opening steps from the first act. It was the masked ball scene, filled with gaiety and confusion. Romeo, seeing Juliet for the first time, is struck by cupid's arrow.

When she'd danced the scene with Ben it had been lively and fun-filled. But Alexei danced the steps like a sleepwalker, never taking his eyes off her face. His spell-binding, soul-binding, jewel-blue eyes held her captive, so that when it came time for her to move towards him, she did so as if in a hypnotic trance. Their first *pas-de-deux* electrified her. It wasn't that he lifted her so high, or that his understanding of her body was better than Ben's. The reverse, in fact. A few times he fumbled, mis-judging her next step or taking her in the wrong direction, so that she found herself struggling to accommodate him, anticipate his moves. But she didn't mind. She felt honoured to be in his arms, and excited beyond her wildest imaginings.

'It's twelve – we should break for lunch.' Ben eagerly switched off the tape. 'Alexei, mate,' he dropped an arm over his shoulders and drew him off to the side. 'Few things to talk about.' Valentina could hear Ben patiently explaining where he'd gone wrong.

'Shall we go find some food?' Carrie cast longing looks at Alexei's retreating back. 'See you in the cafeteria.'

Once outside, she gave a cry of joy. 'Have you ever seen such a dancer? How could you concentrate with seventy kilos of smouldering sex appeal sweating beside you? You must be the original Snow Princess!'

They passed a group of American girls carrying hamburgers.

'Excuse me, where did you get those from?'

'We'll tell you, if you tell us where you've hidden that cute Alexei.'

'So annoying!' Carrie fumed. 'Everyone loves him, except you.'

Valentina swallowed hard. 'There's a cafeteria on the first floor.'

They found it swarming with Americans and a few of the Bolshoi dancers. Ben arrived as they queued for meatballs and noodles, cabbage salad and black bread.

'Why are you being such a pig to Alexei? You ought to be grateful he's stepping into the breach you caused.' Carrie refused the meatballs.

'I think he's two-faced,' answered Ben, piling a mountain of food on his plate.

'With a face like his, two are better than one,' sighed Carrie, grabbing a table. 'Where is the darling now?'

'In the changing rooms. Probably glued to a mirror, moussing his hair and spraying his armpits with love juice.'

'Nasty. You could do with a little of his polish.' She glowered, then, noticing a ripple of excitement, looked up to see Alexei enter the cafeteria. The Americans parted like the Red Sea from the sheer force of his presence.

'Ah, there you are.' He glided over, wrinkling his nose disdainfully at the meatballs on Ben's plate. 'How can you eat something that has passed through the intestines of a dog?'

Carrie and Valentina burst out laughing. Ben's scowl deepened.

'I need more time with you, Valentina. Can we work this afternoon?' Alexei leaned over to her seductively.

'I ... we ... tomorrow Mama arrives. We have so much to do. We move out of the Metropol today; we'll be in the Hotel of the Fallen Heroes.'

'How suitable for our unfortunate Ben here.' He smiled smoothly. 'Then perhaps you and your charming sister could take care of these details while I partner Valentina?' He opened his eyes wide in appeal at Ben.

'I'd love to help out.' Carrie fluttered her eyelashes and folded her arms so that her chest looked bigger.

'Excellent.' He flashed even, gleaming teeth at Carrie and to Valentina whispered, 'I'll see you at two in the studio,' and left.

Ben looked as though a tiger had padded out of the jungle, rubbed against his legs and disappeared before he could fire a shot. 'What a slimy bastard.'

Valentina looked at him sharply. 'Are you jealous?'

'Jealous of that try-hard! He can't even dance; he's all show and no substance. And he's an old ham when it comes to acting – melodramatic and over the top. Watch out, he'll upstage you at every opportunity.'

'Ben!' Valentina was genuinely shocked. 'He was brilliant! Not as good as you yet – he has to learn the steps – but for a first run-through, I thought he was excellent. He has real charisma. If you're not fit by Friday, we'll still have a show, thank heavens. Aren't you pleased?'

Ben hunched down into his jacket, pulled his beanie down to his eyebrows and muttered a single expletive the girls chose to ignore.

Valentina found Alexei later in the studio, practising the solo in which Romeo mourns Juliet. Slipping off her jumper, she took up her position on the floor beside him, feigning death. The polished floor reverberated with his movements, so that she could feel every step and every leap along the length of her body. Soon he was kneeling beside her, taking her in his arms. She breathed deeply, allowing her body to go limp as he carried her to the front of the stage. Her fingertips trailed the floor as he stepped in time to the funereal music. Slowly, she slid down his thigh as he lowered her to the floor, her head coming to rest in his lap. The kiss scene.

Ben always held his lips to hers, stroked back

her hair, then lowered her gently to the floor, almost in one movement. Alexei clutched her to his chest, gripping her shoulders tightly, his agonised features raised for almost a minute. Then, pulling her up towards his face, he kissed her hard, brutally hard, for what seemed like several minutes. Releasing her, he deliberately trailed his fingers over the gooseflesh on her bare midriff, so that when he finally let her go she fell bodily against his thighs, overwhelmed by his passion. Then, leaping to his feet, he let her crash over onto the floor while he danced the final tortured movement before his suicide.

Valentina lay stunned. Her lips, crushed against her teeth, felt bruised and her shoulder ached from landing hard on the floor. The whole scene had frightened and hurt her. She also felt wildly, hopelessly excited.

The familiar bars of music faded as he drank the vial of poison, staggering to rest, dead, beside her.

A burst of clapping rang out. Dazed, Valentina lifted her head to see Carrie rushing towards them.

'Alexei, that was brilliant! I have never been so moved. The passion of the scene – for the first time I understood the character. Poor Romeo, with so much intensity, death was the only option!'

Alexei sprang to his feet. 'For me it is easy, I have always understood passion. It is in the blood of the Tartars.' He held out a hand to Valentina. 'And with a Juliet as bewitching as Valentina here, how could I not feel passionate?' He held out his hand, helping Valentina to her feet, staring intently into her eyes. 'We rehearse tomorrow?'

'Mama will be here then.' Valentina's voice shook.

'And your father. You are still looking for him?'

'We have a clue. Viktor Ivanovich Galliano is my uncle. He might work as a shoemaker to the Bolshoi, as my grandfather did. Or in some related business. I must find him.'

'I go this afternoon to collect shoes; I will inquire. I call you later, at the Hotel of the Fallen Heroes.' He collected his things and left. Valentina watched a thousand Alexeis leave, and felt a thousand times deserted.

'He's in love with you, Val.' Carrie looked devastated. 'And all this time I thought he fancied me . . .' Unable to continue, she fled the studio.

Valentina stood in the centre, staring at herself reflected back from every position – sideways, backwards, front – feeling as confused and splintered as her mirror images. Terrified, she fell back on routine, her answer to feelings she'd lost control of. And for the rest of the day she organised, phoned, ticked lists, counted costumes, argued, cajoled, and worked like a robot – anything to avoid seeing those haunting blue eyes.

That evening, at the Hotel of the Fallen Heroes, there wasn't much to feel victorious about. They chewed their way stolidly through cold potato salad, mutton and a large greasy fish that was mostly head. It eyed them mournfully as they slumped around the table.

'So what if Dr Vlad has vetoed my perform-ance. What would he know?' Ben poked hopefully at the fish bones.

'Only what years of medical training have taught him, which is a lot more than you!' Carrie flung down her English *Woman's Own* magazine. She was in a sour mood, having stewed all after-noon on the inescapable fact that she'd lost Alexei. 'Do you think if I dyed my hair black he'd go for me?' she implored her friend.

Valentina blushed. 'It doesn't matter; he can fancy the whole American *corps-de-ballet* for all the difference it will make to us.' She glanced nerv-ously at her watch. 'Mama will be here tomorrow!'

'She doesn't scare me.'

'She can give us a rehearsal schedule so tight, we won't have time to visit the bathroom.'

Ben looked up from the magazine. 'There is an article here which tells you how to avoid unhealthy relationships.'

'How?' both girls answered at once.

'By finding a decent, incredibly handsome, healthy guy like me.'

'If only you were healthy, we wouldn't have all these problems,' Valentina sighed.

They fell back into the gloom which the ambi-ence of their new hotel only emphasised. It looked like a barracks from the outside, including guards at the door. The cavernous dining room was as desolate and deserted as a mess hall. They were the only guests.

Valentina couldn't eat. The memory of Alexei's mouth against hers had affected her stomach. She felt like the perch on the platter in front, stripped to the bone and utterly helpless. And there was only tonight left; Mama would be here by eight in the morning.

*If only he'd ring*! She no longer cared about finding her father. She didn't think her friendship with Carrie would stop her either. It was as if the adrenalin rush she'd felt at rehearsal had short-circuited her brain. All she could think about was Alexei. *Please ring*, she silently implored. *Call me. Call me. Call me.*

'Miss Valentina Galliano.' The waiter's voice echoed in the empty hall. He approached them bearing a tin tray on upheld fingertips. 'Madame.' He handed her an envelope.

Valentina snatched it up, ripping it open with shaking fingers. 'It's Alexei! He's found someone who knows Viktor. He's coming to pick me up and take me over there.' Crazy with joy, she threw her arms round Ben and Carrie's necks, kissed them warmly and cried 'Wish me luck!'

Like a bird, she flew through the dingy mausoleum of a foyer, then up the cold concrete steps, two at a time, to her room on the first floor. There were five minutes before Alexei came. Five minutes to prepare herself for the most important date of her life!

She didn't pause to ask herself what she was hurtling towards. That would have been like asking the river why it rushed to the sea.

# 8

Valentina pulled on her ruby cashmere sweater and long black boots. For once she decided to let her hair, still damp from a cloudburst, dry loose around her face. Make-up! She must wear make-up, and she only had theatrical stuff. Carrie's room was down the corridor and her door thankfully unlocked. She dashed in and, using the mirror, carefully painted a fine black line around her almond-shaped eyes. And lipstick. Fossicking in Carrie's bag, she found a carmine gloss that slicked on her lips and tasted of raspberries. Stepping back, she could see that the sweater emphasised her pale skin, like a blood-red sunset over fields of snow. Finally she threaded the silver hoops Babushka had given her through her ears. Then, spraying herself with 'Opium', another find in Carrie's bag, she swung her camel coat over her shoulders and set off to find Alexei.

Standing in the foyer, watched by an impassive guard, she felt she'd been waiting for this moment her entire life. He was late, late enough for the anxiety and excitement to reach hysterical proportions. But when he finally made an entrance, he looked heart-stopping in a heavy black wool overcoat and white turtle-necked sweater.

'It's incredible, no?' He took her hands in both of his and kissed her briefly on each cheek. 'I pick up our shoe repairs, ask old Boris if he hear of your uncle and bang! He tells me he know a shoemaker who lives in,' he pulled out a piece of paper, 'Leningradsky Prospekt. We go there now.' He ushered her out into the street and into a van with MEAT written on the side. 'This man work many years for an Ivan Igorovich Galliano, master craftsman. I'm sure this could be your grandfather. I do well, yes?'

A cheeky grin lit up his face, dazzling her. She climbed over a pile of ballet shoes into the front seat of the van. It reeked of petrol and stale meat. Alexei twanged the handbrake and they set off at a dizzying speed. 'My brother's van,' he yelled over the noise of the sputtering engine. 'He is butcher,' he added unnecessarily. 'He let me use it when I'm in Moscow. How did you like my performance this afternoon?'

'Very different to Ben's Romeo.'

Alexei laughed, his teeth gleaming in the dusky light. 'So you like my dancing, but what do you think of me, Valentina? You didn't answer my letter. I was desolate. But you see, you can't escape

Fate. When Orlovsky call me you need a Romeo, I say to myself, we are meant to be together.' He placed his hand boldly on her thigh.

Valentina felt the sweat running down her sides, even though the van was freezing.

'Maybe I come over to Seednee and visit you some time. You find me work, dancing in that ugly shell building on the water, okay?'

'My Mama wouldn't like that,' she answered shakily. 'She thinks Russian men, I mean ... she prefers Australian men, and Australia. She never wanted to come back here.'

'Ah, that's interesting. So she fled Moscow with her baby and her own Mama at the height of her career, and never looked back. No regrets, no homesickness. This is unusual for a Russian.' He screeched to a halt and yanked on the handbrake.

They were outside a dismal block of flats with a stone sculpture of a bare-breasted woman clutching a group of fat children. The plinth read obscurely 'Soviet Mother Soldiers for the Shining Youth'. Alexei strode round to open the van door and help Valentina out.

'Yes. But she never danced again. She opened a school, and I had to be her best pupil. It was as if she wanted me to have the success she never enjoyed.'

'And you, Valentina, do you want it, or do you do it for your Mama?' He stood idly stroking the face and neck of the Soviet Mother.

'I do it for me,' she spoke defiantly. 'At least,

usually. This whole Russian trip was her idea. It had to be *Romeo and Juliet*, and it had to be the Bolshoi.'

His fingers trailed down to the bare breast of the statue. 'So you are a captive of her dreams.'

'In a way.' She stared fascinated at his hands. Behind his blond head the dying sun set fire to a wild cherry tree. Drops of scarlet blossoms lay crushed on the paving slabs by his feet.

Alexei caressed the stone breast, pausing at the nipple. 'You know in wartime it is the duty of every prisoner to escape?'

'I have escaped. I'm here now, aren't I?'

He turned to face her, making love to her with his eyes. 'And tomorrow, when your Mama arrive?'

Bewitched, she stepped forward, her eyes closed, her face turned up to kissed. She was no longer in control of her body or her mind.

'We'd better go inside now,' he whispered, stepping back, 'and find out who you really are. You want that?'

Valentina wanted to cry out with frustration. Instead she followed him meekly into the dark building, dank with cold, feeling only the burning heat of her desire.

Their footsteps echoed harshly as they trudged up several flights of stairs. Somewhere water dripped. Under a bare light bulb, Alexei stopped to bang on a door with peeling brown paint.

An elderly, pot-bellied man with bristly hair opened the door. 'Go away,' he growled in Russian.

Alexei introduced them and produced a bottle of vodka from his inside pocket. The door was set aside and Valentina found herself in a tiny over-crowded room, lit by an oil lamp and warmed by steam from a samovar. Glasses were produced, and the vodka was poured and dispatched before anyone spoke.

'You look for Galliano?'

Valentina nodded eagerly. The old man boosted himself up from his armchair and clawed open a drawer of photographs.

'I think this could be his son.' He pulled out a black and white print from a mahogany box. It showed a pale-eyed man in a fedora, with a jaunty feather tucked into its brim. He laughed happily into the camera, his arm around a woman. It was her mother, many years ago. There could be no mistake about their relationship – they were brother and sister.

'And the woman – Anya. Do you know her?'

'Oh, yes. Oh, yes.' He wound his arms around the back of his chair, eyes narrowed. 'I worked many years for their father. A good man, a great man.' He poured himself another vodka. 'I was a boy when my father apprenticed me to him, the best master cobbler in Moscow. Your uncle also trained; that was before he joined the Communist Party.'

'What did he do in the Party?' She looked anxiously over at Alexei, who was fiddling with the knobs on a battered transistor radio. An old Elvis

Presley song, 'Heartbreak Hotel', crackled out feebly through the static. Satisfied, Alexei sat down again.

'Just an apparatchik. But they liked him; he rose quickly, and in those days that meant he could get things, like food and petrol. Viktor had his own car and an apartment near the Kremlin. He was highly thought of.' The old man pursed his fleshy lips in disgust.

'And my mother?'

'Ah, she was different. So beautiful, in the Aryan way. Tall, fair, a real Moscow beauty. And to see her dance would make a dictator weep. She gave her brother seats for the Bolshoi whenever she was dancing; he always sold the tickets.' He shook his head and poured more vodka.

'How much did they sell for?' Alexei looked up with interest.

'As much as a poor shoemaker like myself would earn in a year.'

'Did you know her husband?' Valentina was growing breathless with excitement.

'I heard she got married.'

'Who to?'

'A man from a village outside Minsk. I only remember because my mother was born there and she knew his family. Dimitriov, I think that was the name.'

'There are thousands of Dimitriovs,' Alexei stated, flicking through the photo drawer.

'Ah, yes.' They all contemplated this gloomy

fact. Alexei poured more vodka all round.

The old man drained his glass like a suction pump. 'But it was rather odd the way she went back to her own village to have her baby. In those days, a young wife would always go back to her husband's village. My mother was all agog expecting her to turn up in Minsk. Ballerinas were the pop stars in those days, you know.' He smiled at Valentina. 'But she never came; she went back to her own people.'

'And where was that?'

'Podolsk.'

'Where's that?'

'Not far from Moscow; about an hour or so.' Alexei looked bored.

Valentina pushed her glass towards Alexei. 'Do you remember anything else about Anya?'

'Oh, yes, oh yes.' He shook his head mournfully. 'Poor thing, such a shame.'

'What!'

'Terrible scandal. She left suddenly. Just before a big show, I think it was Prokofiev, maybe *Romeo and Juliet*. They had to use a stand-in. I saw that show; the tickets didn't sell and people like us got seats because we'd worked on the costumes.'

'In 1979?'

'Probably. It was the year I broke my wrist. I'd just had an order for about two thousand kid slippers from the Academy, and the stitching had to be ...'

Alexei yawned and stood up. 'You've been

very helpful. Got to go,' and he gripped Valentina's elbow.

Valentina stood up. 'What was the scandal about?'

'No idea; I was too busy finding leather. Two thousand kid slippers, that meant four thousand insoles. We used felt from matted horsehair in those days and ...'

Alexei shepherded Valentina out of the door and down the dark steps.

'We didn't thank him,' she gasped breathlessly, struggling to keep up with him.

'No need. He'll chunter on forever with vodka inside him. He'd told us all he knew.'

'That my father was a Dimitriov and my mother left in a hurry.' They emerged into the street; it was pitch black and starting to drizzle. A starving dog nuzzled for scraps in the gutter. 'Oh, God. What kind of a scandal could it have been?' At any other time the information would have horrified her, but at the moment all she could think about was how the streetlight brought out the burning sensuality in Alexei's eyes.

He faced her, hands in pockets, collar turned up to the wind. 'Probably nothing,' he shrugged. 'In those days artists were always going West. Who could blame them? They pay good money in the West. Here we have prestige, but no money. We still live like dogs.' He aimed an absent-minded kick at the cur in the gutter.

'Would you like to live in the West?' Her

heart leapt at the thought. Up until now, she had seen only the futility of loving him.

'Yes. I talked to the New York people; they say there are scholarships for trained Russian dancers. I have an audition. Maybe I go to America!' There was no mistaking the excitement in his eyes.

'Oh.' Valentina's heart fell. The rain flattened her hair and dripped from her nose.

'Or Sydney, if you help me. *Dorogaia*,' he said, opening the van door, 'you are wet. I take you home.'

They drove with difficulty back to their hotel. The van had no windscreen wipers and Alexei had to put his head out of the window to see where he was going. He barely spoke to her and grunted when she asked him questions. Valentina felt numb. He was so unpredictable. One minute he made her feel the most desirable woman in the world; the next, it was as if she didn't exist.

*Never marry a Russian*, Mama had always said. But wasn't it time for her to make her own decisions? She'd been a prisoner to Mama all her life. Alexei said it's the duty of every prisoner to escape.

She glanced over at him. He was staring through the steamed-up window, his profile stern with concentration. Her stomach churned with love. She would do anything for him, give up everything for him – if only he'd ask.

Her hand crept over to cover his as it gripped the gearstick.

'We go back to your place?' he asked, smiling across at her, teeth gleaming in the dark.

'If you want.'

'Is very dangerous in Russian hotels. Nationals are not allowed in. They arrest me.'

They drew up at the kerb. A doorman looked up suspiciously from the street booth outside the Hotel of the Fallen Heroes.

'Which floor are you on?'

'The first floor.' Surely he could hear her heart thudding.

'Go in. Go up to your room. Open the curtains, lift the window and switch on the light. I'll be there in fifteen minutes.'

'How will you get in?' Her hands shook as she fished in her pocket for the room key.

He pulled out another bottle of vodka from the back of the van. 'The old guy looks thirsty,' he said, nodding at the doorman.

She tried to lick her lips, but her mouth was bone dry.

He took her hand, lifting it to his lips. 'Everything will be all right now.' Hypnotic, bewitching eyes glittered in the dark. 'Everything, everything, everything.'

Valentina fumbled for the door handle, tripped over her coat hem, and rushed past the doorman without a backward glance.

An old beige carpet muffled her steps as she hurried to her room. No sign of Ben and Carrie. No light under their doors either, thank heavens. She slipped off her coat and crept into the en-suite bathroom, not recognising her face in the mirror. The light of the single bare bulb gave her an unhealthy, agonised expression, like a police mug shot. With shaking hands, she switched on the shower lever. Fumbling with zips and buttons, she ripped off her clothes and stood trembling under the shower.

*Keep calm, breathe steadily.*

Soaping herself and breathing lavender perfume, she felt herself growing calmer.

Finally she wrapped herself in the hand towel provided, and padded over to the window. It was a single sash window, stiff at first, then giving way too quickly. The cold air rushed in, triggering another attack of trembling.

Feeling vulnerable in the light, she fell to her knees, looking for a nightdress. The midnight-blue satin slip she'd bought in Budapest lay at the bottom of her suitcase. It slithered out and lay shimmering on the carpet. At least she was prepared. She slid the nightie over her head and dived into bed, pulling the blankets up to her chin.

Somewhere, not far away, a distant express train hooted. Directly above her the baleful yellow eye of the light bulb glared down at her. There were stains on the ceiling that could have been soot, or splashes of grease. She focused hard on the blotches – anything to stop her mind ricocheting from Australia to Russia, to Budapest, to Ben, to Viktor, to Carrie, to Mama, to her father. Anything to avoid thinking of Alexei and what was about to happen.

A slight rustle from outside. Then she heard sandstone crumbling, and saw his hands on the window ledge. The next moment, he swung himself into the room, switched off the light, and began to take off his clothes.

The curtains were still open and moonlight illuminated his shoulders and chest as he shrugged out of the sweater. He sat down on the edge of her bed, taking off his shoes.

'*Dorogaia*,' he murmured, 'you still worry about your Papa? There is no need.' He stood up, facing her, unbuckling his trousers. 'Your search is over. I am here.'

'I don't understand.' Her voice came out a scared whisper. She could smell him – a faint musky scent.

'I will find him.' He slid into bed beside her. 'I will go to the village of Podolsk.' He took her in his arms and cradled her tightly along the length of his body. One hand stroked the hair away from her face; she could feel the other tracing the curves along her spine and bottom. 'If you were born there, my Valentina . . .' His lips touched hers, opening her up to him.

She melted into his arms. The trembling she'd felt before intensified, only this time lit by the intense heat of wanting him.

'. . . then your birth will be recorded in the village register,' he murmured huskily, pushing her away from him so that he could watch her face. 'Does that make you happy, *dorogaia*?'

Valentina nodded, wanting him to kiss her again. 'But being here with you makes me even more happy.'

'Of course,' he smiled, 'and tomorrow, I dance as your Romeo.' He kissed her neck, slipping off the silken strip of satin on her shoulder. 'And you will be my Juliet.'

He slipped up her nightdress. 'Now I make love to you. Is what you want, yes?'

Weak with pleasure she nodded, lifting her chin, giving herself up totally to the sublimity of his kiss, giving herself to him.

Someone rapped urgently on the door.

Alexei froze. 'Who is that?' he whispered.

Valentina dragged herself unwillingly back to consciousness. 'I don't know.'

There was fear in Alexei's eyes. 'Call out, ask them what they want.' He lifted himself gently up and out of the bed, reaching for his clothes.

'What,' she croaked. She coughed then tried again. 'What do you want?'

'It's only me, Ben. Can I come in?'

She stared terrified at Alexei. 'What should I say?'

Alexei's face hardened. 'Is he your lover?'

'No, of course not.' How could Alexei think that? 'He's my friend. We've danced together for years, since we were nine.'

'Are you okay in there?' Ben's voice grew louder.

'That noise will bring up the security guards.

They break in here and arrest me,' Alexei scowled. 'He is jealous of me; he must have been watching your window. He must have seen me enter. Now he's laying a trap with the guards.' He quickly pulled on his pants and sweater.

'He's not like that. Ben would never do that,' she pleaded.

'All men are the same.' His magnificent sensual lip curled. 'I cannot stay. It is dangerous; I do not trust this Ben. You do not understand Russia. When you have a jealous enemy, like this Ben here, it is easy for them to destroy you.'

This was getting absurd. Valentina felt she was talking to her Mama. 'Ben is *not* your enemy.'

'I take his job, I take his woman; you think he loves me now?'

'Vally, what's going on, mate?' Ben hammered loudly on the door, twisting the handle which squeaked like a car alarm.

'You see?' Alexei's eyes glittered dangerously. 'He cause a commotion deliberately. He knows I'm here. I see you tomorrow.' Clutching his shoes and jacket, Alexei tiptoed to the window and slithered over the sill, disappearing into the night.


'*Valentina*!' Ben roared, rattling the handle furiously.

Rigid with fury, she leapt at the door and flung it open. Ben lunged forward, tripped and rolled over onto the carpet. Unable to stop herself, Valentina

**122**

kicked him with all the strength she could muster. The force of the blow on her bare foot sent her stumbling to the bed in pain.

'You fool,' she groaned, 'you imbecile, you wretched, miserable specimen of low life. Oh, oh, oooh . . .'

Suddenly the dam burst. The flood gates opened and the pent-up frustrations of a lifetime erupted. Valentina, who had never once in her entire orderly, 'Snow Princess' life ever raised her voice, caused a scene, misbehaved or lost control, now rolled around hysterically on her bed, howling like a madwoman.

Ben sat up in shock, helpless with disbelief.

# 9

Ben sat tentatively on the edge of Valentina's bed and stretched out a hand nervously to the shuddering back. Long gasps for air had replaced the terrible howling sound that he found so distressing. He was used to Carrie's histrionics, but they never lasted. And she would usually jump up and laugh at one of his jokes after a few minutes. Right now he could think of nothing funny to say.

All he'd wanted to do was talk to Val about tonight. He was dying to know whether she'd found out anything about her father. In fact he'd fallen asleep waiting for her to come in, but a sound outside his window had woken him up. Then he'd seen her light on, gone to get them both a hot chocolate from the kitchen, failed, and come back to find her light off. But he knew she couldn't be asleep so quickly.

He tried stroking back her hair, tangled on the

cover, but she wrenched her shoulders away and curled herself tighter into a ball. The temperature in the room was lowering. He looked at his watch. One minute after midnight. Madame would be here today.

'Is there anything I can do?' he tried. 'Get you a drink? More tissues?'

A hand crept out to reach for a fresh tissue. She blew her nose and immediately convulsed again with tears.

Ben decided to get her into bed anyway. Picking her up like an injured puppy, he whipped back the blankets and wrapped her inside the bed, tucking the bedding tight around her body.

'Is it something I said or did?' he asked miserably.

'Ughooo.' A muffled sound from under the pillow.

'Was that a "no"?' Ben took off his jumper and laid it on top of her still shaking back.

'Is it a girl's thing? I could go and get Carrie. . . '

'No!' She whipped off the pillow and glared wildly at him with scarlet cheeks, damp black curls and glittering eyes. Ben had never seen her look so incredible. And that nightdress! He was horrified to discover himself wanting her.

'Don't you dare tell Carrie about tonight. Nothing happened anyway.'

'Does it have something to do with Alexei?' Ben was sure it couldn't be. In fact he guessed it must be seriously bad news about her father, something so awful she couldn't even talk about it.

'It's better to talk about these things. Come on Val, it's me. Your best friend.'

'But you're a male.'

'So?'

Valentina blew her nose again. Through chattering teeth, she said, 'I'll never see him again.'

So it was about her father. He must be dead. Ben's kind heart bled for her.

'Would you like a cuddle?'

Valentina nodded her head, terrified the tears might start.

For several minutes he held her wrapped in his arms, rocking, patting her back, making soothing noises. He was struggling to come to terms with a variety of feelings he'd never experienced on a surfboard.

'He came to visit me tonight, in my room.'

'What! Your father?'

'No! Alexei.'

Ben wrestled with this new idea. 'What for?'

'To make love to me.'

Outraged, Ben assumed the worst. 'The sleazy bast ...'

She stiffened in his arms, then pushed him away. 'I asked him to! I'm not a child, you know,' and she buried herself back in the pillow. 'You think I'm not interested in men, you and Carrie with your Snow Princess jokes. It never occurred to either of you that I might have feelings as well.' A

126

torrent of sobbing washed over her, louder and stronger than before.

'And ... you ... disturbed ... him ... and ... he left! He probably thinks I'm an inexperienced, immature baby. He's probably given up on me.' Valentina spoke in gasps, painful shudders racking her body.

'You mean I disturbed him when I knocked?' Ben didn't know whether to laugh or cry. He handed her more tissues. 'Of course he'll come back. *I* would! Anyway, you can't second-guess what he thinks, and it wouldn't matter if you could. It's what you think yourself that counts.'

'I don't know what I think,' Valentina wailed, suddenly realising how true that was. 'All I ever do is what other people want.' Fresh sobs.

'Oh.' Ben looked up hopefully. 'Then maybe you let Alexei into your room because you were trying to please him. Did he talk you into it?'

'No! I'm in love with him, Ben. I've never felt like this before. He's the most wonderful person, he makes me feel like a real woman.' The tears abated as she relaxed, remembering his touch.

'What do you like about him?' Ben was gobsmacked with disbelief and jealousy. A wild boar with rabies and seven-inch quills would have made a better bedmate!

'His dancing,' she sighed.

Ben blinked in disbelief.

'His courage, you know, on the train.'

Ben bit hard on his tongue.

'His intelligence.' She sat up, rubbing her eyes. 'Do you know, he's found a way to track down my father? You see, tonight we discovered I was born in Podolsk. It's a small village not so far from here. The records will have my father's name on the certificate. Isn't he brilliant? He said he'd track it down tomorrow ... before you burst the door down and chased him away.'

Ben opened his mouth to speak, but thought better of it. She'd calmed down and the last thing he wanted was a fresh outburst.

'And if Mama lets him,' she continued. 'She may insist on rehearsals all day. They'll be here soon.'

They both contemplated this bleak fact.

'How are you feeling?' he asked, stroking the hair off her face.

Valentina smiled weakly. 'Getting there. God, I've been stupid! All these years struggling to please Mama. I've never even had a boyfriend. When Alexei kissed me, it was like a new world opening up. I couldn't bear him to stop. Do you think I should defy Mama and carry on seeing him when she's here?'

'And did he?'

'What?'

'Stop! Did he stop what he was doing when I banged on the door?' Ben raised his voice.

'Had to, didn't he? Anyway, what do you think about Mama? You've always encouraged me to defy her.'

'Yes, but with Alexei?'

'I know what you think. But you're wrong. It's Fate. We're meant to be together. When I'm with him, it's like I'm not in control any more, I'm lost in something, it feels incredible.'

'That kind of feeling is often just body heat, lust. It doesn't last.' Ben took the argument as far as he could go, biting back the desire to scream 'No! Don't do it!' at her.

'This isn't lust.' Limpid eyes gazed up at him – mysterious black pools he was in danger of drowning in.

'And I've just realised something else. Talking to you made me see it.' She flung her arms gratefully around him.

'What was that?'

'I have to trust myself. I have to find out what I want and think. You see, all my life, I've let Mama make all the decisions. I just assumed she knew better than me. And she'd given up so much for me. I thought I was being a dutiful, respectful, good little Snow Princess. You guys were right.' She smiled shyly up at him through tear-soaked eyelashes.

Ben felt a surge, like electricity, roaring through his body. He longed to reach down and kiss her lips, pink and swollen from crying, inches from his own. He turned his face away in pain.

'But the truth is I wasn't being Miss Perfect for anyone but myself. I've just been too scared to branch out on my own. Hard work and obedience has been a perfect cover for cowardice. I've never taken responsibility for my own decisions. Don't you think it's time I grew up?'

Ben could only nod in dumb agreement.

She yawned and stretched. 'I think so too. I'll be able to sleep now, thanks to you. You've been fantastic.' She ruffled his hair and snuggled back into the bed.

Ben stood up. 'Just one thing,' he asked, gazing down at her lace-covered breasts. One of the midnight-blue straps was slipping off her shoulder. 'Did you wear that tonight for Alexei?'

'Mmm.' Valentina stretched luxuriously. 'Do you think I look good in it?'

Ben made a strangled sound and backed out of the room. 'Night, Val,' he whispered.

'Ben,' she called, her voice husky from crying, 'I love you so much. You're my best friend in the world.'

Lying back contentedly, she heard the door click shut. She switched off the bedside light and lay gazing at the moon. It was a sharp new moon, like a silver fingernail. *It is the duty of every prisoner to escape.* She remembered Alexei's naked body silhouetted in the moonlight.

*A new moon, a new me.* Her mind roamed briefly to what 'a new me' could be, short of having Alexei as a boyfriend, but she was too tired and emotionally drained for any more self-analysis.

Her eyelids fell and she sank like a stone into unconsciousness.

**130**

A sharp, unfamiliar buzzing dragged her awake the next morning. Fumbling for the phone, she was jolted by her mother's voice.

'Tina-lina! My precious, we arrive. I come up to your room now.'

Valentina sat bolt upright. Leaping out of bed, she caught sight of herself in the mirror. Her eyes had disappeared behind folds of puffy red skin. Her nightdress looked downright slutty. Clothes from her suitcase spilled out over the floor, right up to a strange fur hat. Alexei's! Panic-stricken, she moved into fourth gear, like a speeded-up movie, flicking things under the bed, dragging on an old tracksuit and splashing cold water on to her face. She was still in the bathroom fighting with the rusty pipes when the door banged.

'Coming, Mama,' she yelled, zipping up the neck of her tracksuit top.

The door flung open, and there stood Mama, dressed like the heroine in *Doctor Zhivago*. 'My little one,' she exclaimed, engulfing her in a perfumed, furry embrace. 'How *ghaaastly* this place is.' She homed straight in on the one thing Valentina had missed. The window from last night was still open a fraction.

Madame yanked it hard down. 'So cold in here, and dangerous. Give those savage Russian boys an inch, and they'll prise your window open a mile. Now.' She turned, settling herself grandly on the bed to light a cigarette. 'You must tell me everything. Orlovsky say you have a problem.' She drew deeply on her cigarette. 'What *prrroblem*?' Madame rolled the 'r' so hard the word sounded like a plane taking off.

'Nothing serious,' Valentina quailed. Then, remembering her resolution from the night before, she took a deep breath and rushed it out. 'Ben had a bit of an accident and we're rehearsing a stand-in just in case but it will probably be all right and in any case the stand-in is a final year at the Kirov, their principal boy, and he's done Romeo before so it's all right.'

Madame froze. 'I see.' Ice filled the air.

'Are the others here?'

'Yes.' Madame stirred herself. 'Come, we talk about this later. We have much to do. Much, much more than I anticipated. And, Valentina, take those earrings out. You look like a gipsy.'

Valentina followed her mother downstairs to the vast gloomy dining room, where a crowd of excited dancers were drinking coffee and crowding around Carrie and Ben. Ben looked haggard. He stood up and smiled weakly when he saw them.

'I talk to you later, Ben.' Madame cut him dead, then swept off, screeching in Russian to the waiter about the coffee.

'What's she saying?' Ben whispered.

'She just said, "Take away this bilge water, you useless nose-picker".'

'I meant about me.'

'Nothing. Just looked at me and snapped into action.'

Valentina was right. Madame said nothing at all about the stand-in. But she ordered Ben to stay away from rehearsals that day to give Alexei a chance to develop his own Romeo, just in case he did have to perform. And she announced there would be a full technical rehearsal starting at ten. Valentina had to accompany her to the Bolshoi immediately to help set up; the others, led by Carrie who knew her way around, must arrive at nine-thirty. Everyone grumbled, but dutifully set about finding their rooms.

By nine, there was only Ben left, hunched miserably over a cup of cold 'bilge water'. Valentina saw him as she stood in the foyer waiting to leave with Mama.

'How's the wrist?'

'Vlad'll be here soon. It'll be okay.' He pulled down his beanie and folded his arms.

'I'm so sorry.' Valentina bent down to kiss his cheek. 'Look, Alexei is nowhere near as good a dancer as you.'

'That's not what you said last night.'

Valentina was caught. The truth was that she really wanted to dance with Alexei tomorrow; but Ben was her closest friend and she felt disloyal saying so. 'I was still mad at you. And over-wrought. I guess I'm more like my mother than I realised.' In the distance, she could see Mama fussing at the reception desk.

'I got such a shock, seeing you like that. You've always been so orderly and controlled.'

'Maybe I've changed.'

'Don't change too much.' He smiled at her. 'And, Val, what's the name of that village?'

'Shh.' Valentina glanced nervously at her mother. 'Podolsk. What are you thinking of doing? You can't read Cyrillic or speak Russian.'

'I've got a spare morning; Alexei won't be off the leash all day. I might as well have some fun playing detectives.' A loopy, toothy grin lit up his face. 'Maybe do some snowboarding, that sort of thing.'

'Idiot,' Valentina laughed, giving him a quick hug and darting out at the sound of her name.


Rehearsals began at exactly ten. There was a different atmosphere at the Bolshoi as soon as Mama arrived. Orlovsky couldn't kiss her hand enough. Props and Wardrobe snapped to attention, the Americans forgotten. A rheumy-eyed old man in administration remembered her Juliet from the seventies and fell to his knees to kiss her foot. It seemed the 'scandal', whatever it may have been, was completely forgotten. Valentina saw how classical dancers are worshipped in Russia. Even the young State dancers had heard her name and paid their respects. Alexei introduced himself confidently, bowing low and murmuring reverentially about how honoured he was. But Mama hissed sideways at Valentina, 'Don't trust him!'

By the time they had all dressed, and warmed

up and were standing ready in the wings, Mama had taken her place in the auditorium with Orlovsky. At exactly ten, she raised her eyebrows at the pianist and Act One began.

The opening scene is set during a masked ball in the House of Capulet, Juliet's family. Some of the dancers wore their masks to get the feel of them. Valentina stood in the wings, straining to see Alexei make his entrance. He wore a black crow-feathered mask, looking dangerous and exciting at the same time. She noticed the girls taking extra long to 'greet' him, their backs and necks arched, smiles lingering.

The scene portrays the mutual attraction between Romeo and Juliet that sets the tragedy in motion. They had to convey a sexual tension strong enough to justify the suicide scene. No problem there, thought Valentina, setting off on cue towards Alexei. He stood centre stage staring at her. Unsure of his reaction after last night, and unable to read his expression, she stumbled and fell awkwardly into his arms.

'*Dorogaia.*' He murmured the Russian for 'darling', the endearment he'd used last night in her bed. Valentina recovered her balance and moved smoothly into their first *pas-de-deux*, but her confidence was sapped. The touch of his hands on her body and the heat from his limbs affected her senses. If anything, she wanted him more now than last night, and her longing for him weakened her concentration.

Crowd scenes separate them, and Juliet darts anxiously around, looking for her Romeo. She hears that the man who has captivated her is a hated Montague, but that only increases the intensity of her desire. They stare entranced at each other across the crowded room. Valentina remembered the saloon car on the train from Budapest. Alexei had called their meeting Fate, a once-in-a-lifetime sense of destiny. And she understood Juliet totally. Swooning, she became Juliet, captivated by her enemy, powerless to resist the attraction, determined to risk everything for him. She danced as if she might never see him again. And when Mama called a midday break, she fell exhausted onto a couch in the Green Room.

The girls crowded around her.

'Who is he?'

'Where did you find him?'

'Poor Ben has no chance against that gorgeous Romeo.' The troupe crowded round, desperate to hear the gossip. Valentina tried to fend off the questions. But then the door flew open and Alexei entered, pausing to scan the room. He was instantly surrounded by adoring fans. She tried to catch his eye, but he seemed to be totally engrossed, and when Mama joined them for 'notes', she was sure he tactfully avoided looking at her. After all, he knew how Mama felt about Russian men. Privately, she added 'sensitive' and 'discreet' to his list of attributes and felt grateful.

During the afternoon, they rehearsed the

second act, the famous deathbed scene which had affected her so powerfully the first time they'd danced. Alexei wore no mask this time and she felt even more strongly the attraction between them. There was an increasing potency in his Romeo characterisation. It was if he knew his power over her, and used it to fuel his own performance.

By five that day, most of the dancers were exhausted. They'd travelled for twenty hours before this rehearsal and were on the point of collapse. Madame called a halt and gave call times for the next day before taking Alexei aside. About to leave, Valentina sat down to untie her shoes and eavesdrop.

'I believe you are from the Kirov,' she began imperiously.

Alexei bowed low over her hand and kissed it, murmuring compliments.

She brushed him aside impatiently. 'You will dance tomorrow if called?'

Alexei bowed again.

'Then should it be necessary,' she said quickly in Russian, hoping no one would understand, 'I want to make several things clear. First, you will not dominate my performance with your ludicrous posturings and theatrical mannerisms. They owe more to the *Commedia del' Arte* than to classical ballet.'

Valentina froze in disbelief.

'Secondly, the love scenes with Juliet are met-aphorical only. You have taken them to the point of indecency. I abhor such displays of vulgarity.'

A group of dancers passed by chattering and laughing, drowning out the 'thirdly'.

'And lastly, one move in the direction of my daughter off-stage will ensure you never dance in this theatre again. Is that understood?'

Valentina escaped without hearing Alexei's response. Her cheeks in the changing room mirror were fire-engine red. Her heart beat a thunderstorm. *How could she! How dare she!* For once she questioned her mother's artistic judgement. Everyone could see how magnificent he was! Mama was allowing her protectiveness to cloud her judgement. But that was no excuse for abusing Alexei. She shuddered with embarrassment. What must he think of Mama, of her family – of all Australians, particularly Ben, after last night. *He must absolutely hate me now!*

Feeling wretched and nauseous, she showered, changed, and waited miserably in the foyer with the rest of the troupe. Her heart was hardening against Mama. There was no sign of Alexei, no chance to talk to him and apologise. She wrapped her coat tightly around her and huddled in the corner till Mama appeared.

'Ah, we are all here?' She wafted out of the lift on Orlovsky's arm. 'I go out for dinner. The bus will be here directly.' Without even looking at Valentina, she swept down the steps and out towards a chauffeur-driven limousine.

'You mad at something?' asked Carrie.

'That cow!' Valentina glared at her mother's retreating back as she disappeared into the limo.

Carrie gasped in astonishment.

'And you might as well be the first person to know. Alexei and I are in love, and it's not just a crush.' She glowered, daring her to comment, but Carrie said nothing. She already knew she'd lost her chance.

A single-decker bus, belching carbon monoxide, rattled up. Valentina darted in and took the single seat at the front, pushed her hands in her pockets and stared moodily out of the window. Moscow had never looked so beautiful and out of reach. The old woman selling violets by the corner gave her a toothless grin and waved. A dying sun glittered from the cupolas of the Kremlin and the ancient fortifications of Pokrovskiye Gate loomed up, impregnable and heartachingly beautiful.

When the old bus finally trundled into the gates of the Hotel of the Fallen Heroes, she saw Ben waiting forlornly in the car park for them. The bags under his eyes had deepened, but he smiled bravely at the exhausted dancers.

'Val, come with me.' He steered her in ahead of the rest. 'Got something to cheer you up.'

'Nothing will cheer me up. Mama has just told Alexei never to see me again, and rubbished his work on stage as well. And you know how sensitive he is about his performance.'

'Oh.' Ben wrapped his arms around her and held her tight.

'I'm so tired of her running my life. I feel so wretched.' The tears started again, not the hysterical sobbing from last night, but a steady stream of heartbroken misery. 'After tomorrow I may never see him again. All I wanted was one last time with him.'

'What?' Ben sounded startled. 'Like last night?'

'Help me, Ben. Tomorrow afternoon, we break up at two, so that we can all rest for four hours before the show. It's my last chance to talk to him. I know I can persuade him to think of coming to Australia. I just need time. Will you cover for me?'

Ben ran a hand through his tousled, wheat-coloured hair. He looked as though he hadn't slept for a week.

'Please, Ben.'

'Sure,' he croaked.

'What's wrong? What did Vlad say about your wrist?'

'Oh, good news; it's fine.'

'Then it's even more important I see Alexei tomorrow. As soon as the show is over, he'll leave for Kirov.'

'Good. I mean, I've got good news for you.'

'About my father?'

'I went to Podolsk, took some photocopies. Can we go to your room?'

Valentina slumped against him and let him lead her upstairs. Thank God for Ben. At least she had no secrets from him, and he was always on her side.

Ben showed her a copy of her birth certificate. 'It's all in squiggle, but you can read it.'

'Too tired,' she yawned. 'I'll show it to Alexei tomorrow, if he'll talk to me.' Somehow, it didn't seem so important any more. Nothing mattered more than her longing for Alexei. She pushed Ben out, recovered the fur hat from under the bed, stripped off her clothes and crawled under the blankets, hugging the fur tight to her chest. The long silky blond tips stroked her cheeks and played against her lips. A strong, musky, exotic smell clung to the fur. What was it he'd said? *Look no further, I'm here.* He was right, he was all she needed. Oh, Alexei, *dorogoy.*

# 10

'You've got a limp wrist,' said Carrie at breakfast the next day. 'I don't care what Vlad said.'

'There's nothing limp about me.' He looked worried under the bravado.

'Ben.' Madame rapped from the head of the table. 'Thank heavens you are well. The Kirov has gone to the dogs. The lead they sent us would never have carried the role. No discipline!'

'I thought he was excellent,' one of the younger girls offered.

'So does Valentina.' Ben picked gloomily at his sweet roll. 'Where is she, anyway?'

'Shh. Gone to make a phone call,' Carrie whispered. 'She's here now.' They looked up to see Valentina, shoulders slumped, trailing dejectedly towards them.

'How did it go?' Carrie was anxious to make amends. Valentina's outburst yesterday had shocked her, and she felt guilt-ridden for having failed to see how affected her friend had been by Alexei.

'He's left for the Bolshoi already.' But Valentina was sure he was at home, refusing to take her call. And who could blame him, after Mama's warning? Valentina had slept badly, tormented by nightmares. She'd sent out thousands of pink balloons to no avail. After a lifetime of being in control of her feelings, this terrible aching for something and someone unreachable was killing her.

'You two look ghastly.' Madame bore down on Ben and Valentina. 'Is the tension too much for you? You must not worry, this is just a performance like any other. Try to forget where we are. Come.' She moved towards the foyer. 'I hope that useless peasant turns up. At least we have an understudy, even if he does dance like a love-sick duck.'

They gathered their things and followed her out to the bus.

'Hey, it's not the end of the world if it all ends now. Better to have loved, they say.' Ben didn't sound convincing.

'You've never been in love. What would you know?' Valentina didn't mean it unkindly, but she spoke too sharply.

'How would I know; right!' He glowered at Valentina, taking her bag and throwing it into the luggage hold. 'But I do know how he's going to react to being the understudy on top of what Madame said.'

'Mama's not important any more. I'm not giving up on him.' She marched onto the bus, sitting well away from everyone, hunched down into the seat.

But Ben was right. Alexei stood mutinously in the wings as they began the final full dress rehearsal. She tried to catch his eye, but he froze like an alabaster statue, his proud profile turned contemptuously away. He listened in silence as Madame told him Ben would dance Romeo. But the look he shot Valentina told her that he thought she was responsible in some way.

'I must talk to him,' she thought frantically as she moved through the first scene with Ben. 'I have to make him see no one can stop us being together if we want to be.' The 'if we want to be' was a grey area. She was sure now of herself, but as she glimpsed his cold figure in the wings, her heart failed. He looked so angry. Did he still want her?

It was towards the end of the first act that it happened. Valentina had executed a series of turns culminating in a *grand jeté* which Ben was supposed to hold before lifting her high and locking his arms as he walked downstage. She felt a moment's weakness as he caught her, then as she stretched upwards his right arm collapsed and she half-fell back into his arms.

'Damn,' he cursed under his breath. 'Are you okay?'

'Take that from the beginning,' Madame rapped.

'I'm fine; what happened?' But Valentina knew. 'It's your wrist, isn't it?' she whispered

Ben didn't answer.

'Vlad didn't clear you, did he?'

'Look, Val, it's just a sprain – it's nothing.'

'Stop playing the bloody hero, Ben.' She was furious.

'I'm not playing the hero,' he snapped back. 'I just made a mistake, that's all. I'll be fine and . . .'

'When you two have quite finished blaming each other, I'd like to get on with this. It's supposed to be the Final Dress.' Madame moved up a notch from impatience to anger.

Valentina stepped forward and addressed the auditorium. 'Ben can't dance, Mama. His wrist gave way.'

'Traitor,' Ben hissed.

'Is this true?' Her voice boomed out of the shadows.

Ben nodded, glaring at Alexei in the wings.

Madame didn't miss a beat. 'From the beginning of the *adagio*, Mr Ivanoff,' she called frostily to Alexei, who was already in position.

Valentina didn't have time to feel sorry for Ben. She was lost in the sensation of Alexei's hands on her waist. She breathed in the exotic cologne he used, drank in the beauty of his strong torso tensed beside her.

There was no break between acts, no time to speak to him – not with words anyway. So she put every ounce of her feelings into the dance. And she felt him respond. As they stood shaking with exertion between scenes, halfway through the second act, she found the courage to break the ice.

'Alexei,' she whispered.

'*Dorogaia*,' he murmured automatically, keeping his eyes forward, waiting for their cue. Sweat rolled in tiny rivers down his temples. She longed to kiss them away.

'I must talk to you, this afternoon,' she panted. 'Can we meet?'

'Why not?' he answered, tightening his grip on her hand, and rushing them both forward to a great orchestral swell of violins. As easy as that, as if nothing had happened. He's forgiven me, she thought, not sure quite what she was guilty of. Thank God! Every touch of his hand now felt like a promise. A particularly moving *pas-de-deux* became enriched with meaning. Her doubts were cast aside as he swept her along in his energy and magnetism. And when he kissed her on her 'deathbed', she had to fight to control her reaction, to stay limp and unresponsive.

They walked three times through the curtain-call routine, then Mama called her downstage.

'Is beautiful, my Tina-lina, but in the *pas-de-deux* you are not concentrating. Stay focused. You must hold the centre spot, not move aside for Romeo. He is a secondary figure in this scene. He exists only to show off Juliet's beauty. Now take charge, show some command on stage, don't be a –

what does this Ben say – "wuss", okay? Now go, get changed and rest this afternoon.'

Valentina ran to the changing rooms. *Don't be a wuss!* Odd Mama should say that to her now; they were her own thoughts exactly! She was just about to take command, only Mama wasn't going to be too pleased by the result. She found Alexei surrounded by adoring girls in the corridor outside. He shrugged charmingly when he saw her, but made no move to get rid of them. Valentina waited patiently until he finally sauntered over.

'Will you pick me up at two from the hotel?'

Alexei looked blank. 'But your Mama will explode like a warhead if she see me with you.' He raised her hand to his lips.

'I must talk to you. About us.'

Alexei dropped her hand and ran his fingers through his hair.

'Wait. Remember you said you would help me find my father?' She gazed pleadingly up at him.

Alexei folded his arms and nodded over her shoulder at a group of girls passing.

'I have his name at last,' she continued. 'Nikolai Alexandrovich Dimitriov. We found it from the village records, like you suggested.'

Alexei looked interested. '*Nikolai Alexandrovich Dimitriov?*'

'You know him?'

'It could be the "Freezer Czar" – if it's the same Nikolai Alexandrovich.'

'Will you pick me up?' Anxiety welled up

inside her chest. If he refused because of Mama she'd never forgive her, ever.

'Of course. I must help you find your father.' He stroked her cheek and ran his finger over her lips. 'I promised to and I always keep my promises. I go now and make enquiries.'

A shiver ran down Valentina's spine.

'Be ready for me. I come at two.' Then he leant forward and brushed his lips over hers.

By the time Valentina opened her eyes, he was gone. Jubilant, she showered and scampered off to the bus, barely noticing Ben's haggard face as he sat with Carrie enduring one of her palm readings.

'I can't find your marriage line,' she squealed. 'Looks like you'll be single and have billions of girlfriends.'

'That'd be right.' He snatched his hand away and stared moodily out of the window.

'Only trying to cheer him up,' she told Valentina, who had taken the seat behind them. 'Did you make it up with Alexei?' she whispered.

'Carrie,' she leant forward conspiratorially, 'if anyone asks, I'm asleep and not to be disturbed this afternoon.'

'That's a hell of a risk.'

Valentina blushed. 'We're going out. It's not what you think, unfortunately,' she giggled.

'Be careful, Val. I know he's gorgeous. But he knows it too. Guys like that aren't serious about love.'

Valentina sat back, lips tightened. Carrie as

**148**

well? She was supposed to be her friend! Well, what could she expect? She'd won Alexei and Carrie was just as jealous as Ben, for different reasons. How tiring people were. As long as she did what they wanted, all was well. The minute she didn't, it was carping criticisms. To hell with them. She had Alexei.

Sitting in the meat van, bumping along the cobbled medieval road through Nikitskiya Gate with Alexei, was as close to sheer bliss as she could imagine. Spring was bursting through in the parks and window boxes. Oak trees lining the boulevards splashed livid green against the grey sky. She hoped Nikolai Alexandrovich lived in the beautiful old part of Moscow. She also hoped he wouldn't be there. This was her day, hers and Alexei's. She'd resolved in her mind to speak to Mama as soon as the show was over. If Mama couldn't help Alexei into Australia, then she'd find another way. She smiled over at him lovingly. He'd been as high as a kite since he'd picked her up, singing snatches of opera in a surprisingly high-pitched tenor.

'Your father lives in Rublovo-Uspenskoye Street. Is the richest part of town. How do you like that? Your papa one of the *élite!*' His eyes shone, blazing blue, engulfing her in light.

'He may not be my father.' She smiled indulgently. Surely his excitement proved he cared!

'I make enquiries. This Dimitriov was married

to a Bolshoi dancer, many years ago. You see?' He laughed out loud and revved the engine.

On a corner, by the traffic lights, a group of waifs scrambled up from the pavement and surrounded the car, dirty faces pressed to the windows, hands outstretched in supplication. What beautiful children, thought Valentina, admiring their luminous dark eyes, framed by ebony curls tumbling over their shoulders. She reached in her bag for roubles.

'Don't,' he ordered. 'They're only gipsies. You'll encourage them.' He rolled down his window and yelled, 'Back to your rat holes, little pissers!'

'Now.' They turned the corner into an ugly avenue of square granite houses set back behind three-metre-high iron railings. 'We are here!'

Valentina stared, disappointed. 'Are these houses? They look more like new office blocks. How could any one family want so many rooms?' There was something depressing, even frightening about the rigid monotony of the architecture.

'Magnificent, aren't they? Your father is worth something, let me tell you.' Alexei took her hand warm in his, softly stroking her palm.

'So is he the "Freezer Czar"?' She wasn't sure she liked the idea, picturing a Lenin-like figure carved from ice.

'Indeed he is.' Alexei rolled down his window, his eyes fixed eagerly on number sixty-six. 'The secretary at his office address was very informative.'

'For a bottle of vodka?'

'No, not in her case,' he grinned, 'but she told me all about Nikolai Alexandrovich Dimitriov. It seems he left Moscow soon after you and your mother. But in his case he disappeared to East Germany. I suppose the KGB wanted to punish him for Anya's defection.'

'Poor Papa,' murmured Valentina.

'Nothing poor about Dimitriov. It was the best thing that could have happened. He was a real entrepreneur and set up useful contacts in Germany, importing whitegoods. You know, washing machines, microwave ovens, things like that. After *glasnost*, he came back to Moscow. Now he's the leading supplier of whitegoods in Russia. The rubbish we make can't compete with the Western stuff, and everyone has to buy through him. The man's a genius!'

Valentina tried to adjust to having a wealthy businessman for a father. She stared at the house, hiding behind rusty beech trees. A uniformed guard stood at the gate. 'Has he remarried?'

'Yes. Three girls.'

She felt unaccountably saddened by that fact. 'Then he probably won't want anything to do with me. He has a new family; ours only brought him trouble.'

'Rubbish. You are number one child, Valentina Nikolaiovna Dimitriov. You come first.'

'I can remember him; he had blue eyes like yours, Alexei.' She reached over tentatively, but his hand felt cool. He kept his eyes on the house. 'He won't remember me,' she sighed.

'We go in.' He made to get out of the van.

'No! I've seen enough for now. We have to dance tonight. I need to think about it. Perhaps tomorrow. You know, in a way, meeting you has taken away the urgency I used to feel. Now it's not so important after all.' She searched his face for understanding.

'You are overwhelmed. He is great man. No matter, I go and introduce you. I speak to him, man to man!'

'No, please. I couldn't cope with it right now.'

'This is foolishness, Valentina Dimitriov. You must face up to him and demand your rights.'

'Please, please don't push it. Later, I promise, after the show.'

Alexei's face hardened. 'Okay, let's go; I have appointment this afternoon.' And he snapped down the handbrake and squealed into a U-turn. They drove back to the hotel without speaking.

*What did I do?* thought Valentina, miserable in the silence. There was something about the set, hard line of his profile that terrified her. Fear, love, wanting and denial thrashed around in her stomach like food gone bad. The nasty flavour of bile rose in her throat. He jerked to a halt outside the gate and leaned over to open her door.

'There you are.'

No *dozvedanya*, no smile. Just the cold command to get out. The terrible lump in her throat almost choked her. She hurried up to her room and lay rigid on her bed, fully dressed, staring at the ceiling.

Ben was pacing up and down in the men's changing rooms at the Bolshoi. He glanced at his watch for the hundredth time. He'd been there since six, stretching out with the other dancers for something to do. Alexei hadn't turned up to the warm-up class. Valentina looked haunted, but when Ben tried to speak to her, she assured him everything was fine. Madame had fumed about the new breed of Kirov dancers, the breakdown of discipline, the breakdown of law and order in Russia, and the superiority of all things Western, until they'd all prayed she'd shut up. As guests of the Bolshoi, it was embarrassingly rude to be caught criticising.

Ben picked up a bottle of apple juice and ran it down his cheek to cool himself. The heat of anger was rising inside him. Alexei was jeopardising the whole show. In one hour the audience would be seated and the curtain would rise.

'How ya doin', buddy?' A young American dancer strolled in wearing a tracksuit. 'Left my gear here earlier. You on tonight?'

Ben held up his wrist. 'Stuffed! A dickhead called Alexei Ivanoff is standing in.'

'What, that guy from the Kirov?'

Ben mumbled, unplugging his apple juice and gulping it.

'You'll be lucky. I saw him thirty minutes ago in the other studio, downtown. He's auditioning for the Cultural Exchange Scholarship to New York. Looks like he'll get it, too. The girls are mad about him and our AD's a woman.'

Ben choked. 'You've got to be joking! He's on in thirty-seven minutes!'

'Well, I don't know about you, but it'd take me longer than that to get ready. See ya,' and he disappeared, leaving Ben speechless.

Moments later, Ben was out of his clothes, into the costume and preparing his shoes to dance. There was a knock on the door.

'Everything okay?' It was Madame. 'Thirty-minute call.'

'Okay,' mumbled Ben, trying to disguise his voice.

*'Ne opazdevay!'*

Ben mumbled what he hoped was a suitable response, breathing a sigh of relief as the footsteps receded.

He caked on the fastest make-up he'd ever done, grateful the first scene was masked. At least he could get away without eye make-up. He was just buttoning up the last of the miniature boot-lace buttons on his waistcoat when the door flew open.

'I am here,' announced Alexei without a trace of embarrassment.

'Too bloody late,' swore Ben, hearing the orchestra tuning up.

'They can wait.' He stalked over to the make-up table and sat down. 'Take off my costume.'

'No way, mate.' Ben placed the mask over his head.

Alexei weighed up the situation, then shrugged. 'Well, is only third-rate student production from third-rate country. Who knows about Australia, anyway? The audience will think you are Austrians.'

Ben's fists balled and he took a step towards Alexei as the stage manager called for Romeo. 'I'll be back, mate. We've got unfinished business.'

'You are jealous; I understand.' Alexei finished the rest of Ben's apple juice. 'I take Valentina. Sorry, *mite*.' Sneeringly he imitated Ben's accent.

Ben set off down the corridor, hearing Alexei laugh and call out, 'I take her to New York with me.' The laughter rang in his ears. Ben was not given to violence; he only got involved in fights to stop them. But he promised himself, as he stood waiting for his cue, that the minute the show was over he would allow himself the luxury of punching the lights out of Alexei Ivanoff.

Then with a broad smile, he stepped into the spotlight.

Valentina waited breathlessly. She'd been at the theatre since five, hoping to see Alexei. It had been impossible to rest after he dropped her off. How had she offended? Perhaps she'd been ungrateful. After all his efforts to find her father, she'd shown no enthusiasm. Or maybe he really did have an important appointment and his mind was elsewhere. She must learn not to be so demanding. She bit her lip furiously and summoned up years of discipline. Taking deep breaths into her diaphragm, she consciously controlled her feelings and focused her mind on the performance. The curtain was up on the opening Masked Ball scene, set by the *corps-de-ballet*.

She could see Alexei now, thank God, moving through the crowd of Capulets like a thief in the night. Her knight, her Romeo. When he finally took centre stage, proudly confident of the power of his attraction, she flew gratefully into his arms. The audience gasped, the music changed from major to minor and a soft blue light replaced the full spot mix. Valentina floated in a dream as the familiar haunting melody wove its usual magical spell. She tried to catch his eye, shadowed behind the ornate Florentine mask. There was a new confidence in the way he held her tonight, as if he knew her body intimately, as if they were one person without reference to time or space. She wanted it to go on forever; it had never been so good between them. *He's right, I am foolish, imagining things. He does love me*, she exulted. *He doesn't always show it, but I can feel it now. I can feel it.*

The passage ended. As Juliet, she flew out momentarily into the wings, caught her breath and

156

returned. The lights are up as the Capulets dance the final quadrilles to end the Ball scene. Juliet, relaxed now without Romeo, all her doubts dispersed, throws herself into the gaiety of the dance. An unexpected round of applause greeted the scene. Orlovsky stood in the wings, beaming.

'Such life, my child, such energy and passion. You are your mother's daughter.'

'Thank you,' she beamed, her eyes glittering with joy. 'And Alexei? Wasn't his Romeo wonderful?'

Orlovsky looked confused. 'He didn't dance, my dear. Some kind of fracas. I saw him in the corridor a moment ago. On the ground, I'm afraid, bleeding.' He spread his fingers and wrinkled his nose in distaste.

# 11

Valentina bit her knuckles to stifle the cry rising in her throat.

'Which corridor?'

'Outside Props.'

She thought quickly. Ben must be on stage now, dancing in the Montague scene. Alexei must have been injured before the show started and Ben forced to take his place. *How could I possibly have mixed them up*? She must see Alexei now and reassure herself he was all right, but the only way to Props was across the stage. She could run behind the apron, but the audience would see her silhouette. No time to go downstairs; she had a scene in two minutes. What on earth could have happened to Alexei? *Blood everywhere*! While these thoughts fought for attention like spoilt children, the music changed and the stage manager called 'Balcony scene'.

She rose on *pointe* and floated out towards Ben.

'What happened?' she hissed through a clenched stage smile.

'I hit him.' Ben held her waist while she pirouetted, then came to rest facing him. 'Don't worry.' He spoke like a ventriloquist without moving his lips. 'I only broke his nose.'

She smiled up at him longingly. 'You snivelling pathetic excuse for manhood.'

Ben only heard a mumble through gritted teeth. He allowed her to fall backwards and swooped over her, kissing her firmly on the mouth. The next moment, she was dancing alone in a moonlit spotlight, a Juliet besotted by her Romeo, a perfect expression of the virgin fantasy. The lyrical beauty of the dance is completed when Romeo joins her in a series of graceful steps synchronised to symbolise their unity.

'Sorry, Val,' he breathed as they turned inwards.

'You will be.' Choked with rage and breathless with exertion, she had no energy to think beyond the obvious. Ben was jealous, Ben had resorted to aggression. Alexei had guessed he would.

The first act ended in a storm of applause. As the curtain fell, she turned and ran. The corridor was empty. She found Alexei draped over a sofa in the Green Room, drinking vodka from a styrofoam coffee cup, a plaster across his nose.

'Is broken.' He poured another drink despondently.

'Poor darling.' She knelt at his side, clutching his spare hand in two of hers. 'Ben?'

'I didn't want to fight. What is the point of violence? I'm a peaceable man.' He gazed at her sorrowfully. 'You see, jealousy does strange things to a man.' He sat up slowly, wincing. 'He refuse to take off my costume when I arrive a little late, then I say okay, you dance. Then I decide to watch from the wings, and he come off stage and hit me. No reason!'

'Alexei, I'm so sorry. Are you sure you're all right? Can I get you anything?'

'A mirror.' He staggered to his feet, clutching his side. 'If my profile is damaged, I sue! Has Ben's family got money?'

Valentina was taken aback by the question. 'I've never thought about it.'

'Well, no matter, yours has. We use the best lawyers.'

'We haven't got money!'

'Ah, so you think, little one.' He waggled a finger at her, then hooked a hand round her neck and pulled her into his arms. 'My little Valentina, *dorogaia*. I think maybe I take you to New York with me. I win scholarship. You like that, escape Mama, live with Alexei?'

Valentina sank into his arms in disbelief. Her thoughts raced. She was feeling the heat of his hands through the fine chiffon costume, melting

160

into his body. Her Alexei, really really hers at last?

'You mean that – take me with you?' She would have gone to Siberia with him; New York was a bonus.

'Why not? I must ask your father's permission first. In Russia, it is the custom when you marry.'

'But he doesn't even know me!'

'He will want to know that the daughter he last saw as a child is now a beautiful woman, a great ballerina and wife of the Kirov Gold Medal winner, Alexei Ivanoff, rising star of the New York Ballet.'

Valentina was dumbstruck. A door banged behind her.

'First call, Act Two.'

Her costume; she had a costume change! 'I'll be back. Wait for me!'

Alexei lifted her hand to his lips, his eyes burning into hers. 'I have waited for you all my life. Another hour will not make a difference.'

By the time Valentina had changed and reached the wings, Ben was already on stage, a hand outstretched, waiting for her. This act charts the tragedy of their love affair. Drunk with passion, Romeo and Juliet plan to escape their warring families. As she threw herself into the story, it seemed the perfect solution: escape all the ties of the past, a new beginning, a new life together.

'You look happier,' Ben whispered as they paused momentarily in the wings. 'Am I forgiven?'

'Not sure,' she answered, drawing in a deep

breath and stepping back out into the light.

The lovers' plan misfires when Romeo, against his wishes, is drawn into a fight, killing Juliet's brother. The fight scene was always brilliant. Ben, an excellent sworsdman, almost blinded her with light flashing from his sword. Thank heavens he wasn't carrying it when he'd bumped into Alexei. How extraordinary that he should have attacked like that! And to risk his arm by dancing tonight, just for a moment's glory! Ben always had been impulsive. *Brave but stupid*, she thought, moving out again into the light to mourn her dead brother.

Later, in the wings, she peered tentatively into the audience. She could just see Mama in the front stalls, her face a mask of concentration. She must be terrified of the deathbed scene, she thought – the final dying *pas-de-deux* where Romeo has to carry the dead Juliet. If his wrist goes again, the whole performance will be ruined. Glancing back at Ben, she noticed him dancing with a strange wildness, perfect for a confused young man. He was berserk with love and grief. She'd never seen him dance so well. We'll possibly never dance together again, she thought with a pang.

Finally, they were on together, Valentina lying on the floor as the 'dead' Juliet. It was during this scene that his arm had given way in rehearsal. She crossed her fingers and opened her eyes a slit so that she could watch him. His face was a mask of concentration. Now he approached her carefully and she lay still in his arms as he lifted her safely up. Fluttering her eyelashes, she caught sight of his face close to hers, preparing for the kiss. The expression was infinitely tender. Then she felt his lips on hers, and there was a passion she'd never experienced from him before. Passive in his arms, it was almost arousing to feel the intensity of his desire.

The lights fall and it is Juliet's turn to wake and find Romeo dead. Ben's magnificent body lay stretched out like a sacrifice. Moved, she found real tears falling as she danced her final steps. This is a real farewell she thought, weeping over him, her dearest friend. Leaving him will be like a death. Who else will I turn to in trouble? The poison taken, she slowly fell across his body, her head resting on his chest. 'Oh, Ben,' she murmured, 'I am going to miss you so much.' Violins wailed the final sad bars of Prokofiev's dirge. Her head, on his chest, almost bounced with the pounding of his heart. The lights went out.

'That feels good; don't move,' he whispered as the curtains fell.

'Animal.' She kicked his leg in the dark.

Thunderous applause smashed the silence and banks of lights flooded the stage as the heavy velvet curtains swooped up.

She knew she'd been good, they'd all been good, but she couldn't believe the cries of *bravo! encore*! the stamping feet and the wild clapping. Dripping with sweat and exhilarated beyond reason, she tumbled out with the whole troupe towards the changing rooms.

'Valentina.' Alexei stood in the shadows.

She reached out for him happily. 'How was it?'

'Not now, you have a meeting. Come.'

'No. You were wonderful.' Hurt, she asked, 'What meeting?'

'With your father. I arrange it,' he added proudly, dragging her off down the corridor.

'How? Why? I can't! What does he ... ?'

'You will see. I solve everything.' Gripping her elbow, he shepherded her down the corridors, filled with hysterical dancers high from the performance, musicians in black, and crew laughing and passing bottles of vodka. And maybe that was also Ben she saw, white-faced and staring anxiously after her. Everything passed in a blur.

Alexei turned the handle of a green baize door and pushed her inside. It was a dark, oak-panelled room, rather cold, smelling of cigar smoke. Two people faced her, posed like statues in a *tableau*. Mama, ashen under a rabbit-fur hat. And in front of her a man with the same pale-blue eyes she'd seen in her dreams. But there were heavy bags under them, and his cheeks were blotched red. He looked like the Chairman of the Board, dressed in a dinner suit and starched wing collar. Or a high-living entrepreneur, the type she saw in Sydney around Double Bay and Quayside. The room trembled with his power.

164

'Valentina? Welcome back to Russia.'

It wasn't what she expected. No warmth, no recognition, and no welcome in his eyes despite the smile. Over his shoulder her Mama, crushed with grief, stood twisting a lace handkerchief between scarlet nails. She stared at Valentina nervously.

'Are you my father?'

'No. Your stepfather, or at least I used to be. Come, sit down.'

She fell into an oversized worn leather armchair, slippery with cold.

'Anya, what does she know?' He spoke sternly to Mama. Valentina had never seen Mama so subservient.

'Nothing. I thought it better to tell her nothing.' She hovered near the window, as if contemplating jumping out.

Valentina shivered.

'You are chilled after your exertions. Would you prefer to change before we talk?' His English was good, and Valentina noticed his accent was more German than Russian.

'No. I want to know who my father is now.' She felt her stomach grow numb.

'As you wish.' He settled himself in a chair beside her, pulling out his starched cuffs. Gold cufflinks gleamed dully.

'Can I get you anything? A drink?' He was smooth, urbane, taking his time, almost as if he enjoyed the tension building up. He glanced over at Mama, who was chewing the flesh on the corner of her thumb, and smiled slightly. Valentina decided she didn't like him. The pale eyes were pitiless. Had he always been like that?

She answered boldly. 'I want Alexei with me.'

A gasp from Mama. 'What has he got to do with this?'

'He is my fiancé. He has a right to know what kind of family he is marrying into.' The horror on Mama's face only encouraged her. 'I need him here.'

Dimitriov waved Mama's objections away. 'Ah yes, the young man who visited this afternoon. He didn't tell me you were engaged.'

'We've only just decided.' She carried on recklessly. 'I am going to New York with him.'

A terrible sob rose in Mama's throat. She staggered and fell into an armchair. Dimitriov growled a warning for her to remain silent, keeping his eyes fastened on Valentina, as if she were a specimen under a microscope.

'How interesting. How long have you known your fiancé?'

Valentina faltered. 'Not long; long enough to know how I feel.'

Dimitriov laughed, a short barking noise. 'He is a pretty boy, I admit. And you fell for him? This is priceless, isn't it?' He twisted in his chair to view his ex-wife huddled, glassy-eyed, in the armchair.

'The air is black, Anya,' he rasped, 'with all your chickens coming home to roost.' He returned his attention to Valentina. 'Where is the young man now?'

'Outside.'

Dimitriov leaped to his feet, twisting the door handle. Alexei almost fell through the door, his bandaged nose and sleeked-back hair giving him the look of an eager ferret.

'Come in,' he boomed. 'The lover of Valentina Galliano! Sit over there with your fiancé and we talk.'

A stifled cry of agony from Mama.

Valentina hardened her heart. She nestled back against Alexei as he perched on the arm of her chair, and took his hand for support. 'I want to know everything.'

And Dimitriov told her.

He had first met Anya when he arrived in Moscow as a young man from Minsk, a country boy. She was a student from the Kirov, but such a talented one! Sent to the Bolshoi to join the *corps-de-ballet* when she was only seventeen. A real prodigy. 'I was obsessed with her,' he said simply. 'I wanted to marry her, but she said I was too poor, and in any case, her career came first.

'You know,' he addressed Alexei, 'it takes a woman to inspire a man. Maybe my little Valentina make a man of you yet?'

Alexei flushed, but said nothing.

'When Anya told me that, I woke up. I was like a man possessed. I thank you for that, Anya.'

But Mama kept her face hidden in her fur

collar, her body rigid with disapproval. She'd lost control and abandoned any hope of recovering it.

'*I will move mountains*, I said to myself, *to be worthy of her*. And I did. In those days there was only one way to succeed, and that was in the Communist Party. I became a loyal party member. Sometimes there were unpleasant jobs to do. Give it to Dimitriov – he can smell a bad idea like last week's fish, they said. I did well. They called me "shining youth", gave me a flat, a *dacha* for the summer. I could get caviar and vodka, imported perfume. Eh, Anya, remember the "Evening in Paris", the silk dresses?'

Mama shuddered, hands deep in her pockets to stop the shaking.

'And she was my inspiration: Anya Ivanovna Dimitriov, my wife, the reason for my success. All that I asked in return was a child, someone to carry my name. But she always said next year, after this show or that show.

'What I didn't know is she had a lover.' He picked a speck of fluff from his lapel and flicked it.

'He was a young gipsy. A rootless cosmopolitan, sweating over her in the theatre while I killed myself to pay for her pleasures.'

Alexei withdrew his hand from Valentina's and stood up. Valentina struggled to understand what Dimitriov was saying. What did it mean?

Mama spoke like a zombie, flat and expressionless.

'He was a brilliant dancer; the most talented they'd had since Nureyev. I couldn't help myself. He was kind to me. I turned to him for love when Nikolai was away. He was away on business so much. I never meant to hurt you, Nikolai.'

'So this gipsy is her father?' Alexei turned to Mama, then to Valentina. 'This is why you wear those silver earrings! Gipsy silver. Your father give you!'

'No! Babushka gave me them!'

'Look at her!' Dimitriov raised his voice. 'Does she look like my daughter? I was so proud when she was born. Yet I was a common cuckold. It was two years before I understood that I was the laughing stock of the whole Commissariat.'

'I swear, Alexei, I knew nothing of all this. Mama would never speak to me of these things.'

'Of course, I had to throw my wife out,' continued Dimitriov. 'Any man who valued his reputation would do the same. It wasn't easy. I was heartbroken. Then on top of that, Viktor dealt me the death blow.'

'Viktor – the uncle no one ever told me about!' Valentina glared accusingly at Mama, but she was staring at the carpet.

'Yes, the dunderhead Viktor. Eager husband that I was, I had taken this fool and helped him up to one of the highest positions in the Southern District. And like a scorpion he attacked. He denounced me in the Central Committee, where God knows there were plenty happy to see me fall.

Jealousy is a very powerful motivation, young man,' he warned Alexei.

'He was protecting me.' Mama passed a hand over her face.

'The next thing I knew, I was out.' It was as if Mama hadn't spoken. 'Exiled, in disgrace. They sent me to East Germany. But it might as well have been Siberia to a good party man like myself.' Dimitriov paused to locate a fresh cigar in an inside pocket.

Valentina stared mesmerised at her stepfather. She was trying to picture him with any kind of a heart, let alone a broken one.

'But I survived – more than survived, Anya.' He turned to Mama. 'Pity your brother didn't.' The short bark guffaw came again. It sent a chill down Valentina's spine. 'I still had friends. They took care of him for me.'

'But she is still your stepdaughter,' Alexei interrupted, 'if you never divorced?'

'We must leave.' Valentina started to rise. She had to escape the stale smell of cigars and strange perfume, the malignant chill in the room. And was Alexei accusing her of hiding facts? She had to get away.

'Wait!' Alexei held up his hand. 'I have to know – did you divorce?'

'How could I? Anya fled. Viktor faked the permits. That's how I got him. Counterfeiting – it used to be a capital offence.'

'So you are a bigamist,' persisted Alexei.

'And you are a stupid boy to speak to Nikolai Alexandrovich Dimitriov like this.'

'Valentina is your legal daughter. You owe her.' Alexei held his gaze.

'Owe her what?'

'Support.'

'I owe her nothing! She's the bastard child of a faithless woman.'

'She's still legally your daughter,' Alexei persisted. 'And she's starting a new life with me, in New York. I've heard it's a very expensive capital. She needs a dowry, a suitable dowry for a man of my status.'

The two men stared at each, bulls locking horns.

Dimitriov suddenly laughed. 'So that's your game. You do need discipline.'

'Your world is past. The old thuggery of your generation is over, *comrade*.' He sneered the word. 'But you have obligations here, and I am offering to take them off your hands.'

Valentina could barely believe what she was hearing. She caught Mama's eye. There was a look of shared horror.

'You would sell your grandmother to the highest bidder, shitball. Is that what you saw in little Valentina? A nice fat dollar cheque?' Dimitriov rubbed his hairless chin. 'Well, I must be getting soft in my old age. As a favour to Valentina, who for two years I believed to be my daughter, I'm going to let you leave, without a taste of that thuggery you despise so much. I suppose you prefer the new-style extortion, using women?'

He glared at Alexei, then leaned forward and took Valentina's hands in his fleshy pink ones. 'You were such a beautiful little thing. I'm not your father, but let me give you some advice. Get rid of this dog's breath; you don't need him in your life. Let me get rid of him for you.' His smile was seductive, his tone utterly reasonable.

Valentina heard the green baize door click softly shut. She pulled her hand away, revolted by the soft clammy feel of his skin, his sweet bad breath, that dense musky perfume.

Dimitriov barked, 'Ha! Gone to the toilet. He's had a sniff of his mortality and it stinks of excrement. Let him go, little one. I know his kind.' He stood up. 'I go now too. Anya.' He held out a paw to pull her to her feet. 'History has much to teach Russia. Shall we let it teach us?'

Madame looked at him, ignoring his outstretched hand. 'I can never forget what you did to Viktor.'

'Then we no longer owe each other anything.'

He turned and left.

Valentina stared at a picture on the wall above Mama's head. It showed a group of peasants in the snow, digging for potatoes. She stared at it, imprinting it on her memory, trying to ignore the choking sounds that told her Mama had broken down.

'I want to go home, Tina,' she sobbed. 'Back to Australia.'

'Yes,' sighed Valentina. 'I think I do too.'

Wearily, she made her way back to the changing rooms, numb to the outstretched hands, the congratulations. She barely heard the laughter and the squeals of excitement as the young Australian dancers cleared out the dressing rooms and made for the studio party.

'Coming?' asked Carrie, draped around a drop-dead gorgeous bassoon player from the Bolshoi orchestra.

'No. Is Ben all right – his wrist?'

'Dunno. Stop it!' Carrie pushed away the bassoonist who was clutching at her body, already drunk and out of control.

Valentina thought of Alexei, and wanted to vomit.

'I'm going back to the hotel,' she said, and turned away.

Back in her room, she simply sat on the bed, her mind a blank, for what seemed like forever. It was very late when she at last began to busy herself packing and tidying. Alexei's fur hat still lay on her pillow. She ran downstairs to give it to the doorman, hoping to see Ben. But the foyer was deserted, and the light in his room was off.

She fell into an empty, dreamless sleep, and resented the morning wake-up call. Let me sleep, she thought. I just want to sleep and sleep and sleep.

Next day Valentina went through the motions

of saying goodbye to Orlovsky and the Bolshoi people who came to wave them off. She received compliments graciously, and helped organise transport, tickets, passports and timetables. It was the sort of thing she was good at and could get through on automatic pilot.

On the plane she listened to Ben's version of the events with Alexei with only half an ear. It was all so irrelevant. She was glad Ben's wrist was better; as for the rest, it simply didn't matter.

She did not see Alexei again, and didn't expect to. Dimitriov wasn't the sort of man to bluff. That didn't matter either. Nothing mattered really. Nothing at all.

Neither she nor Mama spoke of their meeting with Dimitriov, or of Alexei, or of New York.

The journey home was nothing. Just a journey.

During the long flight, Valentina went through the motions of talking to her friends, but she couldn't remember what they'd said as soon as they'd spoken. Ben kept close to her all the time, like a faithful Alsatian. He didn't ask questions; he just covered for her when people remarked how quiet she was. For that she was grateful.

But her heart was dead.

Once she reached home, she went to her room and stayed there most of the time. Babushka and Mama whispered behind closed doors. Valentina knew they were talking about her, about what happened in Moscow. At first they asked questions, but she withdrew to her room whenever the subject of Moscow came up. College had broken up for mid-semester, so there was nowhere for Valentina to go. For two weeks she stayed in her room, reading books and listening to music, but mostly just thinking.

The only person she allowed in was Ben. He came over two weeks after they got back.

'I hear you're hibernating,' he said, putting on a Sheryl Crowe CD and lying down on her bed. 'Two weeks is long enough, I think.'

'Take your shoes off,' she scowled.

Ben obligingly removed his trainers and lay back. 'I know what's it like, you know. I once fell in love, I mean really in love, with a girl who wasn't interested in me.'

'You don't think Alexei was ever interested in me?' She picked up the jacket he'd flung on the floor and hung it on the door knob.

'Do you?' asked Ben.

'No.' Her voice was barely audible.

An amazing guitar solo filled the silence.

'How long did it take you to get over it – the girl, I mean?'

Ben half sat up to look at her. She crouched on the floor, hugging her knees, staring red-eyed up at him.

'Maybe never,' he answered.

'Why didn't you tell me about it?' She felt hurt. 'Anyone I know?'

'Yes. But I don't want to talk about it now. I came here to see how you are.'

She chewed her lip and picked at a hole in the carpet. 'Do you remember that horrible fish we had in the Hotel of the Fallen Heroes? That's how I feel. All the flesh has been eaten away and there's just the bare bones of me left. Picked over, eaten away.' She shuddered.

'You'll grow a new body, a stronger one.'

'And there's something else I can't understand. All my life I've wanted to find my father. I thought, if only I had a father, everything would be all right. And now I just don't care. I'm not going to look for him any more. He abandoned me once, didn't he? He's probably just as big a bastard as Dimitriov.'

Ben reached out a hand to her.

'You really loved Alexei?'

She drew in a deep breath, filling her lungs to the bottom. 'I know what you all think. But it wasn't about sex. It was more than that. I wanted to know everything about him.' She rocked back and forwards, one hand tugging a lock of hair, twisting it round her finger and stretching it hard away from her scalp. 'I wanted to *be* him. Does that make sense?'

Ben stared at her. 'Yes. But it doesn't sound very healthy. It sounds too much like the way you were with Mama. Totally under her control, hardly thinking for yourself.'

'Under *her* control; under *his* control. I don't

know any more.' She rocked back and forth almost frenetically. 'I can't seem to make sense of anything. And I'm so unhappy, Ben! It's like a huge black hole inside me.'

'I know.' His voice was husky, sticking in his throat. 'Come here.'

She rose up on her knees, into his embrace. Gently, Ben pulled her up onto the bed with him and held her there in his arms, rocking her, soothing her with heat of his body until, exhausted, they both slept.

'Valentina, we have a visitor.' Mama knocked softly on the door.

Ben yawned. Valentina rolled off the edge of the narrow bed. 'What time is it?' she mumbled.

'Six. Please, let me in.'

'The door's open,' she called, collapsing back on the floor.

'Darling,' Mama spoke softly. Ever since the scene with Dimitriov, Mama had spoken softly to her. 'Ah, Ben, I didn't know you were still here. Well, maybe it is a good thing. She may need your friendship now.'

'Why, what's happened?'

'The visitor ... he is your father, Valentina. Your real father. Come down and meet him.'

# 12

The kitchen was warm, lit by soft lamps and the flames of a woodburner. Valentina and Ben blinked as they adjusted from the darkness of her bedroom. The rich sweet smell of Babushka's famous nut *torte* lingered. Mama and Babushka sat in armchairs on either side of the fire, staring at her nervously.

A man stood with his back to the fire, his hands held out, in supplication, or in readiness to embrace her; she wasn't sure which. Valentina studied his face. His eyes were coal black, deep-set behind hooded lids. His hair was wild, his body sinewy and strong.

'I know you. You watched me rehearsing, at Her Majesty's.'

He nodded. 'I am Sasha Speransky. I was foolish enough to try to speak to you as well. Forgive me for frightening you.' His hands fell to

178

his sides, but he came a step closer, examining her.

Even the curve of his lips was as familiar as her own. Valentina knew immediately that it was true. This was her father. As if a huge jigsaw puzzle had fallen into place, she could now see the whole picture. The picture of her family.

'I was invited to Australia. I came as a guest. Then I see you dancing, and something stirred. I ask your name. Valentina. My mother's name. Only my Anya would have known that. And then I look closer. At first I can't believe, but then I ask questions, I begin to wonder. When your troupe go to Russia, I make a real investigation.'

'I'm nearly nineteen. Why did you never look for me before?' Valentina felt a surge of anger.

'I never knew you were my daughter. Anya told me you were Dimitriov's child.'

Mama spoke quietly. 'Come, Tina, there is much you have to hear. There have been too many lies.'

In the corner, Babushka wept softly into her handkerchief.

'I met your father on stage. We were dancing *Romeo and Juliet* . . .'

Ben laughed out loud.

'I know, I know. The wheel of life; everything returns. You remember when Dimitriov said my chickens were coming home to roost? He meant Alexei had affected you the way Sasha affected me, all those years ago.'

'And how was that?' Sasha took her hand.

'You made me feel alive. You filled me with joy.' Mama turned blazing eyes to Valentina, 'You mustn't judge me too harshly. I was only a child when I met Dimitriov. He swept me off my feet – he robbed me of my willpower. He told me I was nothing without him, and in the end I believed him. But with Sasha, it was very different. We were the same age, students, working each day together. We were comrades. It wasn't until I realised how Dimitriov had enslaved me with his iron will that I knew how much I relied on Sasha's love. I turned to him as a woman. Dimitriov could only give me his passion, but in the end I wanted simple love and kindness. We were like twin souls, is that not true, Sasha? All those years ago?'

'So that is why you never remarried?' Sasha asked.

'Perhaps. But more, I think, because I closed down my heart. Valentina, you have to see that I lived with such fear. When Dimitriov found out about Sasha, and that he wasn't your father, he was like a madman. We were lucky to escape with our lives. I always believed he killed Sasha. Then after we escaped to Australia, we heard Viktor was murdered. For some time, I lost my will to live. Loving was far too hard.

'Then I realised I still had you, and I had to live for you. I wanted you to have the career I lost.' She watched Valentina, searching for under-standing.

Sasha poured a small vodka and handed it

wordlessly to Mama. Ben does things like that, she thought. Looks after me, asks nothing in return. Mama stared, waiting for an answer.

'Mama, I'm glad you lived for me. But I had to live for myself, too, and you never let me. You wanted me to be the next Fonteyn, or the next Galliano. I've lived all my life trying to please you, trying to get your approval. *I never even knew who I was*.

'When I fell for Alexei, it was as if he'd hypnotised me. When I met Alexei, I switched from wanting your approval to wanting his approval. Nothing really changed.'

Mama looked shocked. 'But, Valentina, you always had my love and respect!'

'Oh, Mama, why did you never show it, then?'

Ben left soon after. He'd promised to pick up Carrie from her float-tank session. Babushka made supper, and Valentina sat by the fire with her mother and father, trying to get to know them both for the first time.

Valentina learned she had a half brother at boarding school in England, and that Sasha's wife had died of cancer three years ago. They reminisced about Russia and their life together there. It hadn't all been bad.

'I wanted to marry you then,' Sasha said to Mama. 'Before Dimitriov swept you off your feet. But you were always so remote. You only wanted to be the principal ballerina. You had no time for love.'

'Why didn't you speak?' Mama cried. 'All those wasted years, wasted lives! Why didn't you force me to see how stupid I was?'

Babushka looked up from her knitting. 'No one could speak to you, Anya. There are things in life you have to find out for yourself.'

'Like me with Alexei,' said Valentina. 'I was ready to leave with him. Dimitriov saved my life.'

'And that young man, Ben?' her father asked. 'How do you feel about him?'

'He's my best friend.' Valentina wondered why he had asked the question.

'No more than that?'

'Of course not.' The last thing Valentina wanted to think about was love. 'Tell me more about Russia – when you and Mama danced ...'

It was midnight when Sasha finally left. Valentina stood with him on the doorstep after the others had gone indoors. A fat moon, the colour of a blood orange, hovered low on the horizon.

'Papa.' She kept using the word, enjoying the sound. 'I think I will leave home soon. Take a flat by myself somewhere near the sea.' It wasn't a question, but she looked up at him all the same to see his reaction.

'Well, that is your decision. You have my support, whatever you decide.' He smiled at her.

'Goodnight, *dozvedanya*.' He dropped a kiss on her head. She watched him walk down the path in the moonlight. Her eyes filled up. *My father*.

Because she felt slightly happier the next day, and because it was one of those bright autumn mornings, Valentina decided to get out of the house. Mama suggested they work at the *barre*, but she didn't feel like dancing just yet. She needed sea air to clear her head.

She made for the harbour. As schoolchildren she and Carrie and Ben had spent long, hot summers playing round the coves, darting in and out of the water like baby seals, sucking icecreams and feeding the seagulls. They were some of the happiest days of her life.

But she had another reason for being here. She wanted to look at the cheap beachside units; there might just be one for rent. The more she thought about it, the more leaving home seemed a good idea. She could not go back to being Tina-lina, Mama's Pavlov puppy. Besides, Mama had Sasha now and it looked as though they wanted to get to know each other again. And although she loved Babushka, it was time to look after herself.

A warm wind gusted in from the shore as she got off the bus at Quayside and strolled over to the railings. She stayed for a while, entranced by the sprats feeding underwater around the pilons.

Looking up towards the bridge, she could see yachts and hydrofoils racing across the water, throwing diamond chips into the air behind them. Heavy container ships were being tugged out to sea like massive cardboard cutouts. Even at this late time of year there were still naked children darting around the beached boats on the shore. So much life and activity!

All those years alone at the *barre*, she mused, wrestling with my body. It seems I've spent my life behind closed doors, striving for some artificial ideal of beauty, staring at myself in mirrors. That anxious little face! She took a deep breath of salty air. I just want to live for a while in the moment, she thought. Outside, with the rest of the world. There was a shout from behind.

'Thought that was you!' Carrie joined her at the railing. 'Not so long ago that was us, playing in the sand without a care in the world.' She peered at Valentina. 'How are you?'

'Alive.'

'Want a coffee at Pepi's? Remember how we used to get free chips there when we were little?'

Valentina turned to her friend. 'Yes, in the days when we were allowed to eat chips! Yes, let's.'

They found a seat by the window where they could watch the seagulls. Valentina ordered a muffin and turned it into crumbs to feed the gulls.

'You shouldn't feed them. It only makes them dependent, then they can't look after themselves,'

Carrie spooned up chocolate froth from her cappuccino.

'You're right.' Valentina poured sugar into her coffee. 'I've been crumb-fed all my life. I've decided it's time to leave home.'

'That's excellent! You're starting to recover.'

'In a way.'

Carrie flicked a sympathetic glance. 'Does it still hurt?'

Valentina watched the sugar dissolve and sink beneath the bubbles. 'Yes, a bit. Ben's been through it too.'

A sharp cry escaped Carrie's lips. 'He told you?' She gripped Valentina's hand across the table. 'I was sworn to secrecy, you know, for years. He's loved you for as long as I can remember. I'm so glad he's finally told you.'

Valentina studied her hands, shaking slightly, and held them tight around her cup. The heat burned her palms. Of course! Why was she surprised? She'd always known he cared for her, just as she'd always loved him.

'When you fell for Alexei, he was really cut up,' Carrie continued chattering happily. 'Because Alexei was such a dickhead. Ben never thought anyone was good enough for you.'

'Well, it doesn't matter any more.' Valentina sighed, shaking the last of the crumbs out of the window. She thought about Ben. Always there, always supporting her. And she'd never noticed. It was as if she'd lived her life in a dream and only paid attention to people who hurt her – people like Mama and Alexei. And she'd looked for love from people who didn't exist, like her father.

Carrie stood up. 'I've got to go. I've been up since six helping Ben move out of the caravan.'

'Where is he now?'

'You remember the stone beach cottage at Peaceful Bay? The old fisherman has gone into hospital. He asked Ben to look after his house while he's away. I don't think he realises he won't be coming back.' She added softly, 'Nothing's easy, is it?'

Valentina watched her disappear along the wharf. A poster on the wall opposite showed a bright green frog hopping over the words *You have to kiss a lot of toads to find your Prince*. Smiling, she set off for the bus stop.

She finally reached the cottage as the first few drops of rain splodged down onto her cheeks. It looked derelict from the outside, the garden a tangle of harebells and clover, the gate hanging off its rusty hinges.

'Ben,' she shouted, pushing open the front door. But there was no one there. She wandered from room to room, stumbling over his things, thrown higgledy piggledy over the bare boards. She flung back the curtains, releasing clouds of dust and daylight. No Ben.

In the kitchen, she found a huge framed photograph of herself dancing in *Romeo and Juliet*. It must have been taken in Russia. She turned it over;

the price ticket beside the frame maker's name made her gasp. Ben had paid more than a hundred and fifty dollars! The picture was exquisite, the deathbed scene. As Juliet, her haunted expression mourning her lover seemed too real. Who was she mourning? Romeo or Alexei?

But it looked like Ben beside her, dead for love of her. A wave of guilt flushed through her mind. His beautiful body was like a perfectly sculpted Michelangelo statue. She placed it back carefully in its tissue paper.

The kitchen was filthy. She got to work, clearing the sink, tidying cupboards, scrubbing the floor. And when that was finished, she moved into the bedroom. There was a nail on the wall above the bed. She hung the photograph and stood back to examine it again. So melancholic! *What a tragedy queen I've been*, she suddenly thought with disgust. *Mooning around feeling sorry for myself.* 'Discipline and Obedience!' she said out loud. 'Hah. Just an excuse to avoid feeling anything. Easier to sweat at the *barre* for hours than to face up to the world!'

Angrily, she attacked the bed, ripping off the old sheets and rustling in Ben's suitcases for clean ones. A pile of Ben's family photos lay scattered on the floor – smiling faces, happy groups of young people, his sisters at Christmas, his parents kissing. The familiar black lump in her chest grew tight again.

It was the pain of last week. And that was an echo of the sadness she'd carried all her life. She'd called it 'wanting my father,' when really all she'd wanted was to be loved. She sighed, pushed the hair off her forehead and opened another suitcase. Ben's board shorts, shirts, rashis, goggles and a pile of surfing magazines fell out on to the floor. Carefully, she separated out the clothes and folded them up neatly. The chest of drawers by the bed was empty, so she began to fill the drawers. She picked up an odd shoe from the hallway, scraped up some board wax from the hall table, plumped the newly filled pillows – doing something, anything to stop the pain spreading from her heart. Keep moving. That's what counts. Get everything in order, everything under control, then she'd be all right.

'What are you doing?' Ben stood at the doorway, naked apart from shorts clinging to his thighs. Sea water dripped a puddle on the floor.

'You're making a mess,' she answered, pointing at the floor.

'Why are you tidying up in here?'

'It's what I do. It's the kind of girl I am.' She picked up his jeans and folded them over the back of a chair. 'I talked to Carrie today, something she said ... Then I came here and saw the picture.' She turned round to look at him. There was no need for words. He knew.

He leaned against the door jamb, arms folded, a light twinkling in his eye. 'You've made my bed.' His body glistened with water, his eyes held hers. 'Are you going to lie in it?'

Valentina turned away. She knew this time he

wasn't joking. This time it was serious, and she couldn't treat him like a friendly puppy any more. He was a man, and he loved her. In a way she loved him, but could she handle a relationship after all she'd been through?

'You and I, it wouldn't work. I'm far too orderly and you're a slob. And I never stop worrying. I get depressed sometimes. I still can't stand up to Mama. You said yourself I'm immature ...'

'Crap! Valentina, I know exactly who you are; you can't down-sell yourself to me.'

'We'd fight all the time. I'd drive you mad with my tidiness.'

'We've known each other intimately for ten years and you haven't driven me mad yet. Not totally, that is.'

'I'm not ready yet ... not sure enough of myself after Alexei.'

'Then don't share my bed. But move in with me anyway. We'll take it slowly.' He came towards her.

'I'm scared, Ben.' Her voice was a whisper. 'I'm too scared to feel anything.'

'I know.' He pulled her into his arms and held her against him. On the chest of drawers lay a net bag, bulging with oranges. She could smell the cold salt water mingling with the scent of orange oil.

Still she held back.

'I have to go now.' She slipped out of his embrace. 'I promised Mama I'd be home later.'

Ben turned away towards the bed, then leaned

his head against the window. His shoulders shuddered; he was gasping for breath.

'Ben . . . ?'

'I'm sorry,' he choked.

Alarmed, she pulled him round to face her, then saw he was laughing.

'That picture!' he roared. 'It's Alexei on the floor, not me. I took it at the dress rehearsal.' He broke off into peals of laughter again. 'You don't think I'd let him into our bedroom again, do you?'

'I thought it was you,' she giggled, glad to be able to laugh again.

'What, those chicken legs?' He took it down gently and carried it through to the sitting room.

She called out, 'I'll be back later,' and slipped off down the path, the scent of oranges still in her nostrils.

'I'll expect you,' his voice echoed cheerfully.

Mama was alone in the kitchen when she reached home. She was cooking blintzes for Sasha. A strange transformation was taking place. Mama, who had never lifted a finger in the kitchen in her life, was now chopping and marinading.

'Mama, I want to leave home.' It seemed easier to come right out with it. Since Moscow her fear of Mama had all but disappeared.

Mama rolled a chicken breast around in the snowy flour without looking up. 'Because of Sasha?'

'No. I just think it's time.'

She dropped the chicken into a pan of bubbling fat. The hissing almost drowned out her reply. 'But you will still dance?'

Valentina was horrified. 'Of course. It's my life!'

Mama turned round, a nervous smile trembling on her lips. 'I was afraid it was *my* life. That I'd forced it on you.'

'No way,' she grinned, relieved. 'Look at my genes! You and Papa; what else could I do? Now that I've met him, I feel so much stronger, more whole. I want to move out so that I can grow up. I've lived under your shadow all my life, terrified to upset you, to displease you, to be unworthy of you.

'It was that night on stage at the Bolshoi that gave me confidence in myself. I really understood what I was dancing – I wasn't just a well-trained performing poodle.'

Madame's eyes misted over. 'You were magnificent. If only Sasha could have seen you.'

'He will. There will be many more performances.'

They stood awkwardly for a moment.

'Where will you go?'

'I'll find something, on the beach somewhere. Ben has offered to let me stay with him; he has a cottage now.'

Mama's gaze intensified. 'Will you accept?'

'I'm not sure.'

She took a step forward and held out her arms. 'Valentina, *dorogaia*, you are a woman now; you must do what you think best.'

They hugged each other. The smell of roasting chicken was rich in their nostrils, a bluish haze building up.

'She's burning,' screamed Mama, pulling away to switch off the gas.

'I'm not hungry.' Valentina picked up her coat. 'I have to give Ben my answer.'

Madame looked up from the oven. 'He is good for you, that boy. He was always defending you, always on your side. You could do worse than Ben.' Then she picked up the tongs and rescued the charred chicken breast. 'Good luck.'


The sun was setting when she reached the cottage. The front door was open and the kitchen table was littered with coffee cups, left-over salad, a milk carton, orange peel and bread crusts. Ben was in the shower; she could hear his toneless singing drowned out by squeaky plumbing.

'It's me,' she called out.

'Me who?' he answered.

'I don't know any jokes, remember? I'm the serious one.' She started to clear the table. By the time he came out of the shower, she was in the bedroom, shaking out the duvet, kneeling across the bed to tuck it against the wall. He advanced wearing only a short towel around his waist.

'I've got you now,' he rasped in a Russian accent.

Valentina screamed.

'Vot? You don't trrrust me?' He grabbed at her jacket, ripping it off and hurling it out of the open window. Then he threw himself on top of her, pinning her wrists down on either side of her head.

Valentina, helpless with laughter, managed to burble, 'No, I don't trust you, you're no different from . . .'

But Ben, suddenly serious, let her go and rolled over. 'That's a terrible thing to say to the man who loves you.'

Valentina considered her words. She thought of Alexei, how dishonest he'd been from the start; of Dimitriov, her stepfather who thought nothing of killing her uncle for revenge; of Sasha, who she believed had deserted her.

'Have you come to give me your answer?'

'Maybe I do have a problem with men. I mean, when you think about it, they've all let me down.' She propped her head up on one elbow to look down at his face.

'Is that why you don't want to live with me?'

She nodded. It was strange, but for all their years of closeness, all the memories they had together, there was still the snake in the garden. There was still this fear. 'Even when I wanted Alexei so much I thought I would die, I was still frightened of him.'

'Maybe that was why you wanted him so

much. You never grew up with men; you get attracted to the bad ones. Boring old reliable Ben who loves you more than life itself is a real turn-off.'

She couldn't answer. She watched him get up and close the window. Then he left the room. Music, his favourite, Sheryl Crowe, filled the air – the deep, slow music of love. He came back with a lavender-scented candle.

'Are you getting ready to seduce me?' she giggled.

'I'm trying to act like Alexei.' He closed the curtains and lay down beside her. 'You tell me when to stop,' he whispered, kissing her neck, above the collar bone. Then gently, so gently she barely noticed he was doing it, he unbuttoned her shirt and released the zip on her skirt.

She lay there and closed her eyes, giving herself up to the delicious sensations his fingertips made as they stroked her. This is my best friend, my brother, my father, and my lover, she told herself. He is all the men in my life and the only man I need.

She heard herself say 'I love you'.

Gradually her soul filled up with pure golden sunlight. It was the closest to heaven she could imagine.

Afterwards Ben pulled her closely to him. 'Have you decided yet?'

'How do we know it will last?'

'We don't.' He kissed her firmly.

'But passion can lead you astray. Look what happened with Alexei, and how long that lasted.'

'This is different.'

'I don't trust passion.'

He raised an eyebrow. 'You could have fooled me.' Then he fell asleep.

Later, when the sun had fallen low in the sky, she woke to find him gone. Ripping open the curtains, she could see him down on the beach. A massive bank of charcoal thunderclouds gathered above the ocean churning beneath. Monstrous swells peeled off into three-metre waves. Ben, a lonely distant figure, was preparing to surf. Terrified, she wrapped herself in a towel, and ran down to the shoreline.

'Ben,' she cried, 'I know why it wouldn't work. I'm too nervous. I can't let you go out in those waves! I want to stop you. I'll end up like my mother, controlling you with my fears.'

Ben wondered what she meant by 'controlling him'. What could it mean in a partnership; what was she predicting? Finally he came up with the answer.

'Exactly. That's why it will work between us.' He finished waxing his surfboard and stared out at the swell. It was smashing up hard over by the rocks, but there was still an hour's good surfing left. A sharp wind gusted, lifting his hair and sending a cloud of sand like mosquitos to sting his face. He stared at her through narrowed eyes.

'I love you, Val. We've known each other since we were children. I know you as well as I know the sea. I love being with you, dancing with you.' He leaned forward and caught a curl whipping madly across her cheek in the wind. 'I love the way you imprison your hair in thousands of clips and this bit here always escapes. I love those gipsy earrings. I love the way you keep little lists around the place, and worry yourself silly about forgetting the slightest thing. It anchors me. You keep me grounded. Without you, I could drift out there and never stand on solid ground again.'

She thought rapidly. 'But I hate you taking risks.'

He stared at her steadily. 'What I do will always be my decision.'

'Ben. I find it so hard to trust. The sea, you, my feelings.'

He shrugged. 'What can I say? The sea is my problem. You? Only you can make decisions for yourself. And as for me? I'm a twin, you're my other half.'

Val clutched the towel around her shoulders. The wind was growing colder.

'And yes,' he continued, almost glaring at her. 'There is passion, lots of it, because I like women. No, don't look at me like that. I'm not another Alexei.' He rolled up the wetsuit over his torso, peeling the black rubber over his broad shoulders.

'And if the passion wears off sometime, after a few years, there will still be your tidiness and lists to keep me in line. To control me, if you like. Half your luck there! Now pull up my zip, will you?' He turned his back.

Valentina grasped the big metal clasp in shaking fingers and buzzed it up over his broad back, lifting the hair at the nape of his neck, standing on tiptoes to reach.

He turned to face her. 'Now I'm going to catch that wave out there.' He leaned forward, held the back of her head with one hand, and kissed her hard. Valentina closed her eyes, hearing only the seagulls and the waves crashing to shore, and the pounding of her own blood. She staggered slightly as he released her.

'And that's the end of my story. Whatever you do now, is your decision.' Ben picked up his board and set off towards the ocean. Valentina watched until he grew as small as the cormorants bobbing on the waves.

'My decision,' she murmured, and turned back to the cottage.

# A letter from Isla

Dear Reader,

Thank you for buying 'Bewitched'. Did you like it? It's more romantic than 'Seduced by Fame', partly because mum and I set it in Russia.

Mum did the research for me, I've been flat out with 'Home and Away' and could only scribble away in the evenings.

I particularly enjoyed writing the horrible Alexei. We've all met nasty characters like him. And we're always taken in by them. Once!

When I was small (even smaller than I am now) I took ballet classes and thought myself very romantic. I dreamed of being a dancer when I grew up. Ben, a dancer with the West Australian ballet, told us more about the life of a professional dancer. I must say, it's about as glamorous as working in a TV soap. Not!

I'm working with my mum on the next book, 'Ebony and Amber' about identical twins who are separated at birth. One goes on to become an international supermodel. The other, my heroine, is a tall, ungainly, unemployed motor mechanic. For reasons you'll find out when you read it, they swap places. It's a fun story, but of course still totally romantic.

Thanks for writing back to me after reading

'Seduced by Fame'. I loved your letters and I wrote back to everyone! Phew!

Still, I always like to hear what you think of my books, so do write again if you want to:

Isla's Newsletter
PO Box 388
COTTESLOE WA 6011

All my love,

Isla

# MORE YOUNG ADULT FICTION FROM PENGUIN

☆☆☆☆☆☆☆☆☆☆☆☆☆☆☆☆☆☆☆☆☆☆☆☆☆☆☆☆

### Love Me, Love Me Not   Libby Gleeson

Relationships. Feelings. For the ten Year Eight students who are the central characters in *Love Me, Love Me Not*, it is a time when little else matters. Nine separate stories or one longer tale? Judge for yourself how this new work by award-winning author Libby Gleeson can be read.

*Shortlisted in the 1994 CBC Book of the Year Awards.*

### Wilful Blue   Sonya Hartnett

In this haunting novel, Sonya Hartnett brilliantly explores the intertwined nature of talent and pain, and the mysterious and enduring bonds of friendship, love and memory.

### Sleeping Dogs   Sonya Hartnett

The Willows are a dysfunctional family, and when one of the five children befriends an outsider who wants to uncover their secrets, the family's world is blown apart ... Another powerful and disturbing book from this talented young writer.

# MORE YOUNG ADULT FICTION FROM PENGUIN

☆☆☆☆☆☆☆☆☆☆☆☆☆☆☆☆☆☆☆☆☆☆☆☆☆☆☆☆

### Witch Bank    Catherine Jinks

*'Nobody notices Heather. She may as well be invisible . . . '*

A humorous and quirky mystery with a dash of romance. Set in a large bank, the story is full of shrewd and funny observations about office life and magic.

### Laurie Loved Me Best    Robin Klein

Julia and Andre share an abandoned cottage as a refuge from their lives – until Laurie, a boy on the run, arrives to upset the scheme of things.

### Came Back to Show You I Could Fly    Robin Klein

The moving and powerful story of eleven-year-old Seymour's friendship with the beautiful eighteen-year-old Angie. Beneath Angie's glitter lies the tragedy which is the world of drugs.

*Winner of the 1990 CBC Book of the Year Award for Older Readers. Winner of the 1989 Australian Human Rights Award. Shortlisted for the 1990 NSW and Victorian Premiers' Literary Awards.*
*Now a feature film* (Say a Little Prayer).
*Winner of the 1992 Canberra's Own Outstanding List Award (COOL) Secondary Division.*

# MORE YOUNG ADULT FICTION FROM PENGUIN

☆☆☆☆☆☆☆☆☆☆☆☆☆☆☆☆☆☆☆☆☆☆☆☆☆☆☆☆

**Spider Mansion**   Caroline Macdonald

When the Todd family arrive at the Days' historic homestead for a gourmet holiday, they appear to be the most delightful of weekend guests. But weekend guests should know when to leave, and the Days realise too late that silently they have become enmeshed in a spiralling web of fear.


**Speaking to Miranda**   Caroline Macdonald

On her quest to discover the truth about her mother's death seventeen years ago, Ruby gradually uncovers the answers to her questions – and much more besides.

*Shortlisted for the 1991 CBC Book of the Year Award for Older Readers and the 1991 New Zealand AIM Children's Book Award.*


**The Lake at the End of the World**   Caroline Macdonald

It is 2025 and the world has been cleared of all life by a chemical disaster. But then Diana meets Hector . . .

*Winner of the 1989 Alan Marshall Award, named an Honour Book in the 1989 CBC Book of the Year Awards and shortlisted for the NSW Premier's Award. Runner-up for the 1990 Guardian Children's Fiction Award.*

# MORE YOUNG ADULT FICTION FROM PENGUIN

☆☆☆☆☆☆☆☆☆☆☆☆☆☆☆☆☆☆☆☆☆☆☆☆☆☆☆☆

### Looking for Alibrandi   Melina Marchetta

Josephine Alibrandi feels she has a lot to bear – the poor scholarship kid in a wealthy Catholic school, torn between two cul-
tures, and born out of wedlock. This is her final year of school,
the year of emancipation. A superb book.

*Winner of the 1993 CBC Book of the Year Award for Older
Readers.*
*Winner of the 1993 Kids' Own Australian Literary Award
(KOALA).*
*Winner of the 1993 Variety Club Young People's Talking Book of
the Year Award.*
*Winner of the 1993 Australian Multicultural Children's Literature
Award.*

### Cross My Heart   Maureen McCarthy

A vibrant, passionate, sprawling novel, set in outback Australia.
The story of Mick and Michelle, chasing a dream, crossing their
hearts for the future.

*Shortlisted for the 1993 NSW Premier's Literary Award (children's
books).*
*A Children's Book Council of Australia Notable Book, 1994.*

### Queen Kat, Carmel and St Jude Get a Life   Maureen McCarthy

A wonderfully passionate and absorbing novel about three very
different girls in their first year out of school.

# MORE YOUNG ADULT FICTION FROM PENGUIN

☆☆☆☆☆☆☆☆☆☆☆☆☆☆☆☆☆☆☆☆☆☆☆☆☆☆☆☆

**Sit Down, Mum, There's Something I've Got To Tell You**   Moya Simons

A funny, fast-moving story about Hatty, a teenage girl who thinks her mum needs a love-life after her divorce. Hatty decides to arrange one, with hilarious results!


**The Blooding**   Nadia Wheatley

Seventeen-year-old Col is painfully initiated into the adult world, a world where right and wrong are inextricably linked and painful compromises must be made.

*An Australian Conservation Foundation Book Selection.*


**Shadows of Time**   Patricia Wrightson

A boy and spirit girl befriend each other on a mysterious journey across time, and across the vast continent of Australia. A hauntingly beautiful novel from one of today's greatest writers for children.

# MORE YOUNG ADULT FICTION FROM PENGUIN

☆☆☆☆☆☆☆☆☆☆☆☆☆☆☆☆☆☆☆☆☆☆☆☆☆☆☆☆

### Obernewtyn  Isobelle Carmody

In a post-apocalypse world, Elspeth is one of a new breed of mind thinkers and seeks the truth of her strange powers. A search inevitably leads to the sinister and mysterious Obernewtyn.

*Book One in the Obernewtyn Chronicles. Shortlisted in the 1988 CBC Book of the Year Awards.*

### The Farseekers  Isobelle Carmody

Their refuge, Obernewtyn, is under threat. Only Elspeth and her allies have any hope of resisting the forces of evil. And time is running out.

*Book Two in the Obernewtyn Chronicles. Named an Honour Book in the 1991 CBC Book of the Year Awards for Older Readers.*

### Ashling  Isobelle Carmody

The long-awaited third volume of the *Obernewtyn Chronicles.* Elspeth's old enemy Ariel is back and is seeking revenge, and she herself must finally confront her feelings for Rushton . . . an unputdownable read.

# MORE YOUNG ADULT FICTION FROM PENGUIN

☆☆☆☆☆☆☆☆☆☆☆☆☆☆☆☆☆☆☆☆☆☆☆☆☆☆☆

### Seduced by Fame    Isla Fisher

Isla Fisher, star of the hugely popular *Home & Away*, gives us a glimpse of what really goes on behind the scenes of the glitzy, scandalous world of TV.

### Vicki's Habit    Maureen Stewart

Vicki likes to drink with her friends. She's enjoying herself – so what's the problem? A thought-provoking, very readable look at teenage alcoholism.

### All of Me    Maureen Stweart

Rebecca is fourteen, and dieting. Her goal weight is just thirty-five kilos. This is a moving story of one girl's struggle with anorexia nervosa.

# MORE YOUNG ADULT FICTION FROM PENGUIN

☆☆☆☆☆☆☆☆☆☆☆☆☆☆☆☆☆☆☆☆☆☆☆☆☆☆☆☆☆

**Goodbye and Hello**   Clodagh Corcoran/Margot Tyrrell (Eds)

An innovative anthology of sixteen stories by Irish and Australian writers in which everyone is coming to terms with a goodbye or a hello. An exciting new collection for older readers.

**The Flea and Other Stories**   Peter McFarlane

A collection of eight gritty stories dealing with dilemmas faced by today's teenagers. Uncompromising and daring, the stories are not afraid of tackling problems head on.

**Lovebird**   Peter McFarlane

From this exciting author comes a powerful new collection of unforgettable characters.

*A Children's Book Council of Australia Notable Book, 1994.*